# TRISKELL TALES 2

## SIX MORE YEARS OF CHAPBOOKS

Charles de Lint

SUBTERRANEAN PRESS ❧ 2006

# Table of Contents

Grateful acknowledgements are made to our pal Nina Kiriki Hoffman for letting me put her in a story. Go read her books—she's one of the best.

*for MaryAnn*

# Introduction

*B*ill Schafer (the esteemed publisher of the book you now hold in your hands) has managed the impossible with me: he actually got me to finish this year's Christmas chapbook early. Usually, I'm still writing the story the week before Christmas, then madly laying it out into a printable format and dashing off to the printer with a "please, can you do this in a day" request. You should have seen the looks on their faces when I came in so early this year. Not to mention when I told them I wanted extra copies printed up for Bill's give-away.

But it's all done and the finished book, including this year's story, is in your hands.

There's not a great deal to add to what I said in the introduction to the original *Triskell Tales,* except that yes, six years on, I still manage to get one uncommissioned story written per year.

I like these stories.

They start off as seasonal greetings, but go on, when reprinted, to reach a larger readership than those in my immediate circle of friends and family, and I like that, too. Firstly, because I don't like the idea of my stories remaining "exclusive" or unavailable to my readers. But I also like the sense of the spirit of when these stories were written reaching out beyond the holiday season.

I tend to write from a positive outlook anyway, but these stories— considering how they were written as long "Christmas cards"—are more optimistic as a group than my other collections. I think there's room for such stories—obviously, or I wouldn't be writing them. I also think there's a need for them.

Year by year, the world is turning into a darker and stranger place than any of us could want.

Somewhere, there is always a war.

Somewhere, there is always the threat of an act of terrorism.

Somewhere, there is always a woman or a child in peril.

Nature itself delivers devastating tsunamis, hurricanes and earthquakes.

In the light of this onslaught of shadows, is it naïve to try to shine a little light into the darkness? After all, these stories are only small flashlights of prose and who knows how long their batteries will last.

I don't know. But naïve or not, I will continue to do so for as long as I can find the stories, or for as long as they find me.

I'm a writer. And this is what I do. This is the only thing I do that has the potential to shine a little further than my immediate surroundings.

So these stories are important—to me, at least. Each one is a little candle held up to the dark of night, trying to illuminate the hope for a better world where we all respect and care for each other.

—Charles de Lint
Winter, 2006

# Big City Littles

The Fates seem to take a perverse pleasure out of complicating our lives. I'm not sure why. We do such a good job of it all on our own that their divine interference only seems to be overkill.

It's not that we deliberately set out to screw things up. We'd all like to be healthy and happy, not to mention independently wealthy—or at least able to make our living doing something we care about, something we can take pride in. But even when we know better, we invariably make a mess of everything, both in our private and our public lives.

Take my sister. She knows that boyfriends are only an option, not an answer, but that's never stopped her from bouncing from one sorry relationship to another, barely stopping to catch her breath between one bad boy and the next. Though I should talk. It's all well and fine to be comfortable in your own skin, to make a life for yourself if there's no one on the scene to share it with you. But too often I still feel like the original spinster, doomed to end her days forever alone in some garret.

I guess for all the strides we've made with the women's movement, there are some things we can still only accept on an intellectual level. We never really believe them in our hearts.

The little man sitting on Sheri Piper's pillow when she opened her eyes was a good candidate for the last thing she would have expected to have woken up to this morning. He wasn't really much bigger than the length from the tip of her middle finger to the heel of her palm, a small hamster-sized man, dressed in raggedy clothes with the look of a bird about him. His eyes were wideset, his nose had a definite hook to it, his body was plump, but his limbs were thin as twigs. His hair was an unruly tangle of short brown curls and he wore a pair of rectangular, wire-framed eyeglasses not much different than those Sheri wore for anything but close work.

She tried to guess his age. Older than herself, certainly. In his mid-forties, she decided. Unless tiny people aged in something equivalent to dog years.

If this were happening to one of the characters in the children's books she wrote and illustrated, now would be the time for astonishment and wonder, perhaps even a mild touch of alarm, since after all, tiny though he was, he was still a strange man and she had woken up to find him in her bedroom. Instead, she felt oddly calm.

"I don't suppose I could be dreaming," she said.

The little man started the way a pedestrian might when an unexpected bus suddenly roars by the corner where they're standing. Jumping up, he lost his balance and would have gone sliding down the long slope of her pillow if she hadn't slipped a hand out from under the bedclothes and caught him.

He squeaked when she picked him up, but she meant him no harm and only deposited him carefully on her night table. Backing away until he was up against the lamp, his tiny gaze darted from side to side as though searching for escape, which seemed odd considering how, only moments ago, he'd been creeping around on her pillow mere inches from her face.

Laying her head back down, she studied him. He weighed no more than a mouse, but he was definitely real. He had substance the way dreams didn't. Unless she hadn't woken up yet and was still dreaming, which was a more likely explanation.

"Don't talk so loud!" he cried as she opened her mouth to speak again.

His voice was high-pitched and sounded like the whine of a bug in her ear.

"What are you?" she whispered.

He appeared to be recovering from his earlier nervousness. Brushing something from the sleeve of his jacket, he said, "I'm not a what. I'm a who."

"Who then?"

He stood up straighter. "My name is Jenky Wood, at your service, and I come to you as an emissary."

"From where? Lilliput?"

Tiny eyes blinked in confusion. "No, from my people. The Kaldewen Tribe."

"Who live...where? In my sock drawer? Behind the baseboards?"

Why couldn't this have happened *after* her first coffee of the morning when at least her brain would be slightly functional.

He gave her a troubled look. "You're not like we expected."

"What were you expecting?"

"Someone...kinder."

Sheri sighed. "I'm sorry. I'm not a morning person."

"That's apparent."

"Mind you, I do feel justified in being a little cranky. After all, you're the one who's come barging into my bedroom."

"I didn't barge. I crept in under the door, ever so quietly."

"Okay, snuck into my bedroom then—which, by the way, doesn't give you points on any gentlemanly scale that I know of."

"It seemed the best time to get your attention without being accidentally stepped on, or swatted like a bug."

Sheri stopped herself from telling him that implying that her apartment might be overrun with bugs his size also wasn't particularly endearing.

"Would it be too much to ask *what* you're doing in my bedroom?" she asked. "Not to mention in my bed."

"I might as well ask what you're doing in bed."

"Now who's being cranky?"

"The sun rose hours ago."

"Yes, and I was writing until three o'clock this morning so I think I'm entitled to sleep in." She paused to frown at him. "Not that it's any of your business. And," she added as he began to reply, "you haven't answered my question."

"It's about your book," he said. *"The Travelling Littles."*

As soon as he said the title, she wondered how she could have missed the connection. Jenky Woods, at her service, looked exactly like she'd painted the Littles in her book. Except...

"Littles aren't real," she said, knowing how dumb *that* sounded with an all too obvious example standing on her night table.

"But…you…you told our history…"

"I told *a* story," Sheri said, feeling sorry for the little man now. "One that was told to me when I was a girl."

"So you can't help us?"

"It depends," she said, "on what you need my help for."

But she already knew. She didn't have to go into her office to take down a copy of the book from her brag shelf. She might have written and illustrated it almost twenty years ago. She might not have recognized the little man for what he was until he'd told her himself. But she remembered the story.

It had been her first book and its modest, not to mention continuing success, was what had persuaded her to try make a living at writing and drawing children's books. She'd just never considered that the story might be true, never mind what she'd said in the pages of the book.

# The Travelling Littles

There are many sorts of little people—tiny folk, no bigger than a minute. And I don't just mean fairies and brownies, or even pennymen and their like. There are the Lilliputians that Gulliver met on his travels. Mary Norton's Borrowers. The Smalls of William Dunthorn's Cornwall. All sorts. But today I want to tell you about the Travelling Littles who live like Gypsies, spending their lives always on the move.

This is how I heard the story when I was a small girl. My grandpa told it to me, just like this, so I know it's true.

The Littles were once birds. They had wings and flew high above the trees and hills to gather their food. When the leaves began to turn yellow and red and frost was in the air, they flew to warmer countries, for they weren't toads to burrow in the mud, or bears to hibernate away the cold months, or crows who don't allow the weather to tell them where to live, or when to move.

The Littles liked to travel. They liked the wind in their wings and to look out on a new horizon every morning. So they were always leaving one region for another, travelling more to the south in the winter, coming back north when the lilacs and honeysuckle bloom. No matter how far they travelled, they always returned to these very hills where the sprucey-pine grow tall and the grass can seem blue in a certain light, because even travelling people need a place they can call home.

But one year when the Littles returned, they could find nothing to eat. They flew in every direction looking for food. They flew for days with a gnawing hunger in their bellies.

Finally they came upon a field of ripe grain—the seeds so fat and sweet, they'd never seen the like, before or since. They swooped down in a chorusing flock and gorged in that field until they were too heavy to fly away again. So they had to stay the night on the ground, sleeping among the grain-straw and grass.

You'd think they would have learned their lesson, but in the morning, instead of flying away, they decided to eat a little more and rest in that field of grain for one more night.

Every morning they decided the same thing, to eat a little more and sleep another night, until they got to be so heavy that they couldn't fly anymore. They could only hop, and not quickly either.

Then the trees began to turn yellow and red again. Frost was on the ground and the winter winds came blowing. The toad burrowed in his mud. The bear returned to his den. The crows watched from the bare-limbed trees and laughed.

Because the Littles couldn't fly away. They couldn't fly at all. They were too fat.

The grain-straw was getting dry. The tall grass browned, grew thin and died. After watching the mice and squirrels store away their own harvests, the Littles began to shake the grain from the blades of grass and gather it in heaps with their wings, storing it in hidey-holes and hollow logs. The downy feathers of their wings became all gluey, sticking to each other. Their wings took the shape of arms and hands and even if they could manage to lose weight, they were no longer able to fly at all now for they'd become people—tiny people, six inches tall.

That winter they had to dig holes in the sides of the mountains and along the shores of the rivers, making places to live.

And it's been like that ever since.

In the years to follow, they've come to live among us, sharing our bounty the way mice do, only they are so secret we never see them at all. And they still travel, from town to town, from borough to borough, from city block to the next one over, and then the next one over from that. That's why we call them the Travelling Littles.

But the Travelling Littles are still birds, even if their arms are no longer wings. They can never see a tall building or a mountain without wanting to get to the top. But they can't fly anymore. They have to walk up there, just like you or me.

Still the old folks say, those who know this story and told it to me, that one day the Travelling Littles will get their wings back. They will be birds again.

Only no one knows when.

"You want to know how to become a bird again," she said.

Jenky Wood nodded. "We thought you would know. Yula Gry came across a copy of your book in a child's library last year and told us about it at our year's end celebration. Palko John—"

"Who *are* these people?"

"Yula is the sister of my brother's cousin Sammy, and Palko John is our Big Man. He's the chief of our clan, but he's also the big chief of all the tribe. He decided that we should look for you. When we found out where you lived, I was sent to talk to you."

"Why were you chosen?"

He had the decency to blush.

"Because they all say I'm too good-natured to offend anyone, or take offense."

Sheri stifled a laugh. "Well," she said. "I'm usually much less cranky when I've been awake for a little longer and have had at least one cup of coffee. Speaking of which, I need one now. I also have to have a pee."

At that he went beet-red.

"What, you people don't? Never mind," she added. "That was just more crankiness. Can I pick you up?"

When he gave her a nervous nod, she lowered her hand so that he could step onto her palm, keeping her thumb upright so he'd have something to hang on to. She took him into the kitchen, deposited him on the table, plugged in the kettle, then went back down the hall to the washroom.

Ten minutes later she was sitting at the table with a coffee in front of her. Jenky sat on a paperback book, holding the thimbleful of coffee she'd given him. She broke off a little piece of a bran cookie and offered it to him before dipping the rest into her coffee.

"So why would you want to become birds again, anyway?" she asked.

"Look at the size of us. Can you imagine how hard it is for us to get around while still keeping our secret?"

"Point taken."

Neither spoke while they ate their cookies. Sheri sipped at her coffee.

"Did your grandfather really tell you our story?" Jenky asked after a moment.

Sheri nodded.

"Could you bring me to him?"

"He passed away a couple of years ago."

"I'm sorry."

Silence fell again between them.

"Look," Sheri said after a moment. "I don't know any more than what you read in my book, but I could look into it for you."

"Really?"

"No, I'm actually way too busy. Joke," she added as his face fell. "It was a joke."

"Palko John said we could offer you a reward for your help."

"What sort of reward?"

"Anything you want."

"Like a magic wish?" Sheri asked, intrigued.

He nodded. "We only have the one left."

"Why don't you use it to make yourselves birds again?"

"They only work for other people."

"Figures. There's always a catch, isn't there? But I don't want your wish."

He went all glum again. "So you won't help us?"

"Didn't I already say I would? I just don't like the idea of magic wishes. There's something creepy about them. I think we should earn what we get, not have it handed to us on a little silver platter."

That earned her a warm smile.

"I think we definitely chose the right person to help us," he said.

"Well, don't start celebrating yet," Sheri told him. "It's not like I have any idea how to go about it. But like I said, I will look into it."

"I've decided to give up men," Sheri told Holly Rue later that day.

She'd arrived early at Holly's store for the afternoon book club meeting that the used book shop hosted on the last Wednesday of every month. The book they'd be discussing today was Alice Hoffman's *The River King*, which Sheri had adored. Since she had to wait for the others to get here to talk about it, she kept herself busy talking with Holly and fussing with Snippet, Holly's Jack Russell terrier, much to the dog's delight.

"I thought you'd already done that," Holly said.

"I did. But this time I really mean it."

"Have a bad date?"

"It's not so much having a bad date as, A, not wanting to see him again after said date, but he does and keeps calling; or B, wanting to see him again because it seemed we were getting along so well, but he doesn't call. I'm worn out from it all."

"You could call him," Holly said.

"I could. Would you?"

Holly sighed. "Not to ask him out."

"I thought women's lib was supposed to have sorted all of this out by now."

"I think it's not only society that's supposed to change, but us, too. *We* have to think differently."

"So why don't we?"

Holly shook her head. "Same reason they don't call, I guess. Give me a hob over a man any day."

Sheri cocked her head and studied Holly for a long moment.

"What?" Holly said. "Did I grow an extra nose?"

"No, I'm just thinking about hobs. I wanted to talk to you about them."

Holly's gaze went to an empty chair near the beginning of the store's furthest aisle, then came back to Sheri's.

"What about them?" she asked.

There was now something guarded in the book seller's features, but Sheri plunged on anyway.

"Were you serious about having one living in your store?" she asked.

"Um…serious as in, is it true?"

A few months ago they'd been out celebrating the nomination of one of Sheri's books for a local writing award—she hadn't won. That was when Holly had mentioned this hob, laughed it off when Sheri had asked for more details, and then changed the subject.

"Because the thing is," Sheri said. "I could use some advice about little people right about now."

"You've got a hob living in your apartment?"

"No, I've got a Little—though he's only visiting."

"But Littles aren't—"

"Real," Sheri finished for her. "Any more than hobs. We both know that. Yet there he is, waiting for me in my apartment all the same. I've set him up on a bookshelf with a ladder so that he can get up and down, and got some of my old Barbie furniture out of my storage space in the basement."

"You kept your Barbie stuff?"

"And it's a good thing I did, seeing how useful it's proven to be today. Jenky—that's his name; Jenky Wood—likes the size, though he's not particularly enamoured with the colours."

"You're serious?"

"So it seems," Sheri told her. "Apparently he thinks I can find out how they can all become birds again."

"Like in your story."

Sheri nodded. "Though I haven't got the first clue."

"Well, I—"

But just then the front door opened and Kathryn Whelan, one of the other members of their book club, came in.

"I think I know someone who can help you," Holly said, before turning to smile at the new arrival.

Snippet lifted her head from Sheri's lap with interest—hoping for another biscuit like the one Sheri had given her earlier, no doubt.

"Someone tall, dark and handsome—not to mention single?" Sheri asked after they'd exchanged hellos with Kathryn.

"Not exactly."

"Who's tall, dark and handsome?" Kathryn asked.

"The man of my dreams," Sheri told her.

Kathryn smiled. "Aren't they all?"

Sheri was helping Jenky rearrange the Barbie furniture on the bookshelf she'd cleared for his use when the doorbell rang.

"That'll be her," she said, suddenly nervous.

"Should I hide?" Jenky asked.

"Well, that would kind of defeat the whole purpose of this, wouldn't it?"

"I suppose. It's just that letting myself be seen goes so against everything I've ever been told. My whole life has been a constant concentration of secrets and staying hidden."

"Buck up," Sheri told him. "If all goes well, you might be a bird again and it won't matter who sees you."

"I'd rather be both," he said as she went to get the door.

She paused, hand on the knob. "Really?"

"Given a choice, wouldn't you want to be able to go back and forth between bird and Little?"

She gave a slow nod. "I suppose I would."

She turned back to open the door and everything just kind of melted away in her head. Jenky's problem, the conversation they'd just had, the day of the week.

"Oh my," Sheri said.

The words came out unbidden, for standing there in the hallway was the idealization of a character she'd been struggling with for weeks. The new picture book hadn't exactly stalled, but she kept having to write around this one character because she couldn't quite get her clear in her head. She'd filled pages in her sketchbook with drawings, particularly frustrated because while she knew what the character was supposed to look like, she was unable to get just the right image of her down on paper. Or perhaps a better way to put it was that she didn't so much know what the woman should look like; she just knew when it was wrong.

But now here the perfect subject was, standing in the hallway. Where were her watercolours and some paper? Or just a pencil and the back of an envelope. Hell, she'd settle for a camera.

Though really, none of that would be necessary. Now that she'd seen her, it would be impossible for Sheri to forget her.

It wasn't that the woman was particularly exotic, through there were those striking green streaks that ran through her nut-brown hair. She wasn't dressed regally either, though her simple white blouse and long flower-print skirt nevertheless left an impression of royal vestments. It wasn't even that she was so beautiful—there were any number of beautiful women in the world.

No, there was an air about her, a quality both mysterious and simple that had been escaping Sheri for weeks when she was doing her character sketches. But she had it now. She'd begin with a light golden wash, creating a nimbus of light behind the figure's head, and then—

"I hope that's a pleased 'oh my,'" the woman said.

Her voice brought Sheri back into the present moment.

"What? Oh, yes. It was. I mean I was just…"

The woman offered her hand. "My name's Meran Kelledy. Holly did tell you I was coming by, didn't she?"

Her voice was soft and melodic with an underlying touch of gentle humour.

"I'm sorry," Sheri said as she shook Meran's hand. "I can't believe I've left you standing out there in the hall." She stood aside. "Please come in. It's just that you just caught me by surprise. See, you look exactly like the forest queen I need for this book I'm working on at the moment and…" She laughed. "I'm babbling, aren't I?"

"What sort of forest is she the queen of?"

"An oak forest."

Meran smiled. "Well, that's all right, then."

With that enigmatic comment, she came into the apartment. Sheri watched her for one drawn out moment longer, then shut the door to join Meran and Jenky in the living room.

"I should also tell you that there's a wish up for grabs," Sheri said after she and Jenky had taken turns telling their story.

The two women were sitting at the kitchen table, Jenky on the table in a pink plastic chair. They all had tea—Jenky in his thimble since he didn't like the plastic Barbie dishware, the women in regular porcelain mugs.

"For the one who helps the Littles with this, I mean," Sheri added.

Meran shook her head. "I have no need for wishes."

Of course she wouldn't.

Meran was probably the calmest woman that Sheri had ever met. Neither meeting the Little nor the story the two of them had told seemed to surprise her. She'd simply given Jenky a polite hello, then sat and nodded while they talked, occasionally asking a question to clarify one point or another.

What world does she live in? Sheri had found herself thinking.

A magical one, no doubt. Like the forest in Sheri's latest picture book.

"You can have it," Meran said.

But Sheri shook her head right back. "I don't believe in something for nothing."

"Good for you."

What an odd response. But Sheri didn't take the time to dwell on it.

"So can you help us turn them back into birds again?" she asked.

"Unfortunately, no. Odd as it came to be, the Littles have evolved into what they now are and that kind of thing can't be turned back. It's like making the first fish who came onto land return to the sea. Or forcing the monkeys to go back up into the trees once more instead of becoming men and women. Evolution doesn't work that way. It moves forward, not back."

"But magic…"

"Operates from what appears to be a different law of physics, I'll admit, but that's only because it's misunderstood. If you have the right vocabulary, it can make perfect sense."

Sheri sighed. "So we're back where we started."

"No, because the clock doesn't turn backwards."

"I don't understand."

Sheri might have felt dumb, but Jenky looked as confused as she was feeling and he was a piece of magic himself, so she decided not to worry about it.

"What's to stop the Littles from continuing to evolve?" Meran asked. "Into, say, beings that can change from bird to Little at will the way Jenky here has said he'd like to."

"Well, for one thing, we don't know how."

"Now there I can help you. Or at least I can set the scene so that you can help him."

"I'm still not following you."

"There's an old tribe of words," Meran explained. "Not the kind we use today, but the ones that go back to the before, when a word spoken created a moment in which anything can happen."

"The before?" Sheri asked.

"It's just another way to say the first days of the world," Jenky told her. "Our storytellers still tell the stories of those days, of Raven and Cody and the crow girls and all."

"It was a time of Story," Meran said. "Though of course every age has its stories, just as every person does. But these were the stories that shaped the world and part of that shaping had to do with this old tribe of words."

"A tribe of words," Sheri repeated, feeling way out of her depth here.

Meran nodded. "I can wake one of those words for you," she said. "Not for a long time, but for long enough."

"So you'll just say one of these words and everything'll be the way we want it to be?"

"Hardly," Meran said with a smile. "I can only wake one of that old tribe. You will need to say the words. It's a form of communal magic, which is mostly the kind I know. One person wakes it, another gives it focus."

"But I wouldn't know what to say. Maybe Jenky should do it."

"No, this works better when a human speaks the words."

That gave Sheri pause, the way Meran said the word "human." It was the way humans spoke of other species. She wanted to ask Meran what she was, but she supposed now wasn't the time. And it would probably be impolite.

"So what words do I say?" she asked instead.

"You'll know when the time is right."

"But..."

Meran gave her another of her smiles. "Don't worry so much."

"Okay."

Sheri looked from the magical woman sitting across the table from her to the even more magical little man sitting on a Barbie kitchen chair between them. Jenky watched her expectantly. Meran said nothing, did nothing. There was an odd, unfocused look to her gaze, but otherwise she seemed to merely be waiting, managing to do so without conveying the vaguest sense of pressure.

But there was pressure all the same—self-imposed on Sheri's part, but no less urgent for that.

What if she didn't say the right thing? How much was she supposed to say? How was she supposed to know when the time was right?

It was all so nebulous.

"So when do we start?" Sheri asked.

Meran's gaze came into focus and found Sheri's.

"Breathe," she said. "Slowly. Try to still the conversations that rise up in your head and don't concentrate on anything until you feel a change. You'll know it when you feel it."

Then she slowly closed her eyes.

Sheri copied her, closing her own eyes. Breathing deeply and slowly, she tried to feel this change. Something, anything. Maybe a difference in the air. Some sense that they were sideways from the world as she knew it, inhabiting a pocket of the world where magic could happen.

If magic *was* real, that was.

If it…

She wasn't sure where it originated, the sudden impression of assurance that came whispering through her, calm and sure and secret. She felt like she was at the center of some enormous wheel and that all the possibilities of what might be were radiating out from her like a hundred thousand filigreed spokes. It was like floating, like coming apart and reconnecting with everything. But it was also like being utterly focused as well. She could look at all those threads arcing away from her and easily find and hold the one that was needed in her mind.

"Hope," she said.

"Is that word for them or for you?"

As soon as Meran asked the question, Sheri saw how it could go. She realized that under the connection she felt to this wheel of possibilities, she'd continued to harbour her own need, continued to reach for that elusive partner every single person looked for, whether they admit it or not. He could be called to her with Meran's old tribal word. The right partner, the perfect partner. All she had to do was say, "for me."

Because magic was real, she knew that now. At least this magic was real. It could bring him to her.

But then she opened her eyes. Her gaze went to Jenky, watching her with expectant eyes and held breath.

Promises made. Promises broken.

What good were promises if you didn't keep them? How could you respect yourself, never mind expect anyone else to respect you, if you could break them so easily? What would the perfect man think of her when he learned how she'd brought him to her?

Not to mention what she'd said barely ten minutes ago, how it wasn't right to have something for nothing.

But that was before she'd realized it could really be made to happen.

That was before all the lonely nights were washed away with the promise of just the right man coming into her life.

"No," she said. "I meant faith. Belief. That bird and Little can be one again, the shape they wear being their own choice."

Meran smiled.

"Done," she said.

Sheri felt a rumbling underfoot, like a subway car running just under the basement of her apartment building. But there was no subway within blocks of her place. The tea mugs rattled on the table and Jenky gripped the seat of his chair. Something swelled inside her, deep and old, too big for her to hold inside.

And then it was gone.

Sheri blinked and looked at Meran.

Was that it? she wanted to ask. What happened? Did it work?

But before she could speak, there was a blur of motion in the middle of the kitchen table. Jenky leapt up, knocking his little chair down. He lifted his arms and they seemed to shrink back into his body at the same time as his fingers grew long, long, longer. Feathers burst from them in a sudden cloud. His birdish features became a bird's head in truth, and then the whole of the little man was gone and a grey and brown bird rose up from the tabletop, flapping its wings. It circled once, twice, three times around the room, then landed on the table again, the transformation reversing itself until Jenky was standing there.

He looked up at her, grinning from ear to ear.

Sheri smiled back at him.

"I guess it worked," she said.

A couple of days later, Sheri looked up from her drawing table, distracted by the tap-tap-tapping on her windowpane. A little brown and grey bird looked in at her, its head cocked to one side.

"Jenky?" she said.

The bird tapped at the glass again so she stepped around her table and opened the window. The bird immediately flew in and landed on the top of her drawing table where it became a little raggedy man. Sheri wasn't even startled anymore.

"Hello, hello!" Jenky cried.

"Hello, yourself. You're looking awfully pleased with yourself."

"Everyone's so happy. They all wanted to come by and say thank you and hello, but Palko John said that would be indecorous so it's just me."

"Well, I'm glad to see you, too."

Jenky looked like he wanted to dance around where he was standing, but he made himself stand straight and tall.

"I'm supposed to ask you if you've decided on your wish," he said.

"I already told you—I don't want a wish."

"But you helped us, and that was our promise to you."

Sheri shook her head. "I still don't want it. You should keep it for yourselves."

"And I already told you. We can't use it for ourselves."

Sheri shrugged. "Then find someone who really needs it. A person whose only home is an alleyway. A child fending off unwelcome attention. Someone who's dying, or hurt, or lonely, or sad. You Littles must go all over the city. Surely you can find someone who needs a wish."

"That's your true and final answer?"

"Now you sound like a game show host," she told him.

He wagged a finger at her. "It's too late in the day to be cranky. Even you have to have been up for hours now."

"You still don't get my jokes, do you?"

"No," he said. "But I'll learn."

"Anyway, that's my true and final answer."

"Then I'll find such a person and give them your wish."

With that he became a bird once more. He did a quick circle around her head, followed by a whole series of complicated loops and swirls that took him from one end of the room to the other, showing off.

"Come back and visit!" Sheri called as he headed for the window.

The bird twittered, then it darted out the window and was gone.

"So what's the deal with Meran?" Sheri asked Holly the next time she came by the book store. "Where do you know her from?"

"I had a…pixie incident that she helped me out with last year."

"A pixie incident."

Holly nodded. "The store was overrun with them. They came off the Internet like a virus and were causing havoc up and down the street until she helped us get them back into the Net."

"Us being you and your hob?"

Just as she had the last time the subject of the hob came up, Holly's gaze went to an empty chair near the beginning of the store's furthest aisle, only this time there was a little man sitting there, brown-faced and curly-haired. He gave Sheri a shy smile and lifted a hand in greeting.

"Oh-kay," Sheri said.

She could have sworn there was no one sitting there a moment ago and his sudden appearance made the whole world feel a little off-kilter. She'd only *just* gotten used to little men who could turn into birds.

"Sheri, this is Dick Bobbins," Holly said. "Dick, this is Sheri Piper."

"I like your books," the hob said.

His compliment gave Sheri perhaps the oddest feeling that she'd had so far in all of this affair, that a fairy tale being should like *her* fairy tale books.

"Um, thank you," she managed.

"He didn't appear out of nowhere," Holly assured her, undoubtedly in response to the look on Sheri's face. "Hobs have this ability to be so still that we don't notice them unless they want us to."

"I knew that."

Holly grinned. "Sure you did."

"Okay, I didn't. But it makes sense in a magical nothing-really-makes-sense sort of a way. Kind of like birds turning into Littles, and vice versa."

"So was Meran able to help you?"

The hob leaned forward in his chair, obviously as interested as Holly was. Sheri nodded and told them about how it had gone.

"I understand why you didn't let Meran's magic bring you the right guy," Holly said when she was done. "I mean, after all. You *were* calling it up for the Littles. What I don't understand is, why didn't you use the wish they offered you?"

"Because it's something for nothing. It's like putting a love spell on someone. Isn't it better to get to know someone at a natural pace, work out the pushes and pulls of the relationship to make it stronger, instead of having it all handed to you on a platter?"

"I suppose. But what if you never meet the right guy?"

"That's the risk I have to take."

So here I am, still waiting like an idiot on the man of my dreams.

I don't know which bugs me more: that he hasn't shown up yet, or that I'm still waiting.

But I got to do a good turn and my picture book is done. Meran loved the paintings I did of her as the forest queen. Her husband even bought one of the originals once I'd gotten the colour transparencies made.

What else? I've got a new friend who's a hob and at least once a week Jenky Wood flies up to my windowsill in the shape of a bird, tapping on my windowpane until I let him in. I've got my Barbie furniture permanently set up for him on a shelf in my studio, though I have repainted it in more subdued colours.

So what am I saying?

I don't know. That we all have ups and downs, I guess, whether we bring them on ourselves, or they come courtesy of the Fates. The trick seems to be to roll with them. Learn something from the hard times, appreciate the good.

I didn't really need fairy encounters to teach me that, but I wouldn't trade the experience of them for anything. Not even for that elusive, perfect man.

Author's Note: Sheri's story of the Travelling Littles is adapted from an Appalachian story detailing the origin of Gypsies; I found my version in *Virginia Folk Legends*, edited by Thomas E. Barden. Thanks to Charles Vess for introducing me to this delightful book.

# Refinerytown

*R*elationships are confusing. Actually, life is confusing, but the relationships part of it seems particularly so.

When you don't have a boyfriend, all your energy focuses around the idea of having one. Doesn't matter if the last man in your life was some sorry-assed, miserable excuse of a parasitic worm, or if he dumped you. Doesn't matter that we know we're supposed to be comfortable in our own lives and expect others to be comfortable with us. The idea of having a boyfriend is forever looming on the periphery of everything we do.

But then you get a boyfriend—a good one, mind you—and the funny thing is, you're still not necessarily content. Because now the boyfriend relationship starts looming over all the other ones in your life. Your relationships with your family, your friends, your art…

He talks about having to go away for a bit, and you think, okay, that's sad, but I'll get all this work done. I'll have the chance to gather up the tattered ribbons of semi-suspended friendships and actually spend some time with them.

Except the boyfriend's going away leaves this big hole in your days and everything's still unbalanced.

Like I said. It's confusing.

"So it's just going to be a one-shot," I say. "Unless it really takes off, I guess."

Jilly wheels over to one of the long tables in the greenhouse to put the storyboards I've given her on a flat surface. She's a lot better than she was in the first few months after the accident, but simple things, like holding something large for too long, still aren't possible.

"I like the art," she says as she spreads them out. "It's pretty different from your usual strips. More cartoony."

"That's Nina's influence," I tell her. "She's really into animé—you know, that Japanese animation stuff."

"Who's Nina?" Sophie asks.

"Nina Hoffman. We're collaborating on this comic."

"We met her during the summer," Jilly says. "Remember that book signing you took me to?"

"Oh, her." Sophie grins. "She was fun."

The three of us are in the greenhouse that's attached to the back of Professor Dapple's house. Jilly's been staying with him since she got out of rehab. Sophie moved in to help her out and give her some company. The professor had converted the greenhouse into an artist's studio years ago, when they were both still in university. In those days Jilly shared the space with our friend Isabelle and dubbed it the Grumbling Greenhouse Studio after the professor's cranky housekeeper, Goon. Now Sophie's using it to keep up with her own art. She and Jilly spend some mornings and most afternoons in it. Three mornings a week Sophie takes Jilly to her physio appointments.

"We're calling it 'Refinerytown'," I say. "After those *Bordertown* books by Terri Windling."

Jilly smiles. "I got the reference."

"We were just talking one day—goofing really—but then it all started to click, so we decided to actually do something with it."

"I didn't know Nina wrote comics."

"She helps with the plotting," I say. "And also the background and characters. She originally wanted to pitch it to her editor at Viking—this wild woman named Sharyn November—but Sharyn was so totally not into it. And this from a woman who has chicken puppets."

"Really?" Jilly asks. "She has chicken puppets?"

I nod. Trust Jilly to zero in on that.

"Apparently," I tell her. "Three life-sized ones. She's managed to get out of most of her editorial meetings because they won't let her bring them in with her any more. Nina says she'd have the head poke up over the edge of the table when someone was talking and have the chicken yawn, or make faces at people."

"I think she's putting you on," Sophie says.

"No, it's true. They're like these Muppet chickens."

"I'd love to have a chicken puppet," Jilly says.

Sophie leaves the painting she's working on to look over Jilly's shoulder at the first few pages of the comic that I've finished so far.

"I notice a complete lack of chickens on these pages," she says. "Puppet or otherwise."

"No chickens," I agree. "Just oily fairies."

Sophie smiles. "They're really cute. When you first started talking about fairies that lived in oil refineries…" She shoots me a grin. "Well, I didn't know what to think."

"And those names," Jilly says. "Greasy. Oilpan."

Sophie giggles. "Slick."

"He's my favourite," I tell them. "We're still trying to figure out what his girlfriend's name should be."

"Diesel," Jilly says.

Sophie shakes her head. "No. Squeaky."

"And there has to be a kind of dumb one called Dipstick."

"Thanks a lot, you guys."

"We're just teasing," Sophie assures me.

"I know." I shrug. "But I don't even know how it's going to play out. Probably nobody will buy it."

"I'll buy it," Jilly tells me.

"Nobody I don't know."

"Oh, *pfft*. What's not to like? They're cute. They live in an oil refinery…"

"Exactly. People want their fairies in pastoral, natural settings. Like Brian Froud does. Or Charles Vess."

"People used to like my fairies," Jilly says, "and they just lived in junkyards and alleyways."

"That's because you were a brilliant painter," I say, then my voice trails off as I realize what that must sound like. "Oh, god. I'm sorry. I didn't mean it like that. Like your painting days are forever over."

Ever since the accident, Jilly hasn't been able to paint. Partial paralysis of her drawing arm saw to that. She's been messing around with her left hand, but mostly she just gets frustrated.

"It's okay," she says. "I'm the one who brought it up in the first place."

Sophie walks over to the sink in the corner of the greenhouse and takes three cups down from the low shelf just above it. Filling each with tea out of a thermos, she hands them around to us, then hoists herself up to sit on the work table beside my drawings.

"So why are you doing this comic?" she asks.

I shrug. "I don't know exactly. I guess I want a shot at something more than just writing about myself all the time. That's where Nina comes in. I can't write about myself if we're collaborating on it."

"All the art we do is about ourselves," Sophie says. "Writing, painting. Songs, dance. You name it. If it means anything, there's a piece of you at the heart of it."

I can't argue with that. "I guess I just want to try something that's not so obviously about me."

"I can see that," Jilly says.

Sophie nods in agreement.

"So how's your werewolf boyfriend?" Jonathan asks.

I'm sitting at the counter in The Half Kaffe Café, sipping a latte, and look up. Jonathan has apparently finished reading the latest copy of *Mojo* and now needs some conversational stimulus. I guess since he's the owner, he doesn't have to look busy when there's nothing to do. He's certainly not overrun with customers at the moment. We have the place to ourselves, except for the dreadlocked student sitting at a window table, hunched over her laptop. The new Pink CD's playing on the sound system, the singer telling her diary that she's been a bad, bad girl. I know that feeling.

"He's not a werewolf," I tell Jonathan. "He's a shapechanger."

"And the difference is?"

"He can choose what he wants to be, when he wants to be. And he doesn't have to go around chewing things up during the full moon."

Jonathan nods sagely. He does cool so well, bless his soul, but I knew him as a nerdy little computer geek, heavy into junk food and techno music. That was back in our art school days. The only art Jonathan does now are Photoshopped notices and menus for the café. But the funny thing is, these days he looks like the Bohemian artist he wanted to be in our college days. Slender in his black jeans and shirt, skin clear, mop of blue-black unruly hair, dark eyes no longer hidden behind his old Buddy Holly glasses. Those only come out late at night now, when his contacts start to bother him.

"How come he never changes in front of us?" Jonathan asks.

I feel like going out and buying him another music magazine, but I'm sure he already has every current one. So I try to answer him instead.

"That'd be like you going out with a stripper and us expecting her to dance for us."

"When did I ever go out with a stripper?"

"I said 'like you'."

"But what made you think of a stripper?"

"I don't know."

"Because if you know any strippers…"

"Oh please. Focus here, would you."

Jonathan smiles. "I'm just making conversation."

"Right."

"So where is the wolf man these days, anyway?"

"His name's Lyle."

"Sorry. Where's Lyle?"

"He's out of town. Something to do with his family."

"Which, for him, would be a pack."

"Jonathan," I say, in what I hope's a firm voice. "Would you *please* give it a rest?"

"Okay, okay. I'm resting."

"And for your information, they refer to themselves as clans."

I suppose I should explain this werewolf business.

It's a running joke with my friends—has been ever since I wrote about how Lyle and I met in my comic strip-cum-journal "Spunky Grrl," which appears weekly in *In the City.* I guess every city's got one or more of these weeklies—an alternative press newspaper with show listings, news bits, reviews and columns. I'm in good company here. *In the City* regularly features Dan Savage's column, strips like Dave Russell's "True Monkey Boy Adventures" and Lynda Berry's ongoing sagas.

Lyle and I met right here in the café on a blind date courtesy of the personals—something I don't make a habit of doing, let me add. Though

I guess neither of us has to do that anymore anyway. After a little bit of a rocky start involving a bunch of renegade shapechangers—don't ask, it's way too long a story—we've sort of settled into a nice, relatively normal boyfriend/girlfriend relationship.

The thing is, while regular readers of *In the City* would figure that shapechanger storyline was just me exercising my imagination—of which I've got an excess anyway—my friends all know that only true stuff goes in the strip. Same with "My Life As A Bird," a longer, autobigraphical strip that runs in my own bi-monthly comic book, *The Girl Zone.* The real difference is, the pen & ink-Mona gets to have the last word—you know, like telling the guy off the way you would have when he dumped you, except you couldn't think of what to say until an hour later. The pen & ink-Mona's never at a loss for exactly the right thing to say, though otherwise, both strips do faithfully wander through the ongoing parade of my various screw-ups and mishaps. They have to. Panel after panel of me sitting around drinking coffee with my friends would make for dull reading after awhile.

"If 'Refinerytown' works as well as I think it will," Nina says, "I've got some other fun ideas."

We're talking on the phone about a week after my visit to the Grumbling Greenhouse Studio. It's late at night for me, but still before midnight for her in Eugene, Oregon. Ever since we've started this project there've been any number of emails, faxes, and phone calls going back and forth between our houses. Tonight we started talking about the JPEG character design for Slick's girlfriend I sent her an hour or so ago. But our conversations never stay on topic.

"Such as?" I ask.

I'm a little hesitant. Nina's a lovely woman to be sure, but she has the wildest ideas. You should read her books.

"It's about this snake named Pelican Bob," she says. "He wants to have wings, but of course he can't because he's a snake."

"There've been winged snakes."

"Sure. If you're an Aztec god, maybe."

"Dragons are kind of like snakes with wings."

Nina laughs. "Well, of course they are. But I'm talking smaller scale here."

"Ouch."

"Sorry. But you know what I mean. This'll be the small story. Sort of like *The Little Engine That Could,* except it'll be about a snake who can't."

You see what I mean? And she talks like this all the time. Good thing she's a writer and gets to let that stuff out onto the page. Otherwise she might find the men in white coats knocking on her door.

"So have you heard from Lyle?" she asks.

"He called earlier. He says he's bored, but he sounds like he's doing okay."

"You miss him, don't you?"

"Sure. I'm supposed to, aren't I?"

"That's a funny way to put it," she says.

"I'm just confused," I tell her. "Boyfriends make everything so complicated, both when you have them and when you don't."

"Do you love him?"

"It's not that. It's more…I have this image of myself as an independent woman and it drives me crazy that all Lyle has to do is call and see if I want to get together, and I'll drop whatever I'm doing, even if I've got a deadline looming, to go off and see him. Before he was in my life I was always mooning about having a boyfriend. Now I'm always mooning about my boyfriend."

Nina laughs. "I'm sorry," she says. "I'm not laughing at you. But it's kind of funny, when you think about it."

"Oh, I know. It's all so Marie Antoinette. Having my cake and all."

"Have you talked to Lyle about it?"

I sigh. "It's nothing Lyle's doing. He's actually pretty much the most perfect boyfriend I've had. It's me and the constant story of my life that runs through my head."

"Even in 'Refinerytown'?"

"No. That's why 'Refinerytown' is so important to me right now. It's about the only time I'm not inside my head, trying to make sense of what I'm doing and why I'm doing it."

I guess the way my life goes, I should have expected one of these Refinerytown fairies to show up sooner or later. For real, I mean. The way I had a cantankerous sort-of-dwarf move in on me a few years ago, or find myself going out now with a guy that everybody thinks is a werewolf.

Nina and I settled on Diesel as the name for Slick's girlfriend. She's fun to draw—definitely sexier than any character I've done before with her hourglass figure and flirty ways. The way the whole story starts is when this trollish guy named Crude who lives under one of the fractionating towers—the place where the crude oil is separated into more useful compounds—thinks that Diesel's interested in him. She's not, of course, but it starts a chain reaction of events that allows us to fill our thirty-two pages of comic book with a fun, rollicking story.

So it's late at night and I'm sitting at the drawing board, laying out the panels for my next page. This is the one where Slick and Oilpan are spying on Diesel to see if she's really going to meet Crude at this midnight rendezvous the way Crude has boasted she is. What they don't know is that Diesel's best friend Ethane is spying on them and—

"Ahem."

I sit up with a start at the sound of someone clearing their throat. I look around, but I'm still alone in my studio, which is really just one end of my living room.

"Down here," a strange, small voice says.

My gaze follows its husky timbre to the top of my drawing desk and there she is, sitting on a bottle of Calli ink.

"Whoa," I say. "I've been working way too much on this."

Because standing—well, sitting—there, at a height of no more than eight inches, is Diesel. Not the Diesel I've been drawing. She's got the knee-high motorcycle boots with all the buckles and zippers. The black jeans and the torn T-shirt to show off her midriff. The hourglass figure and the heart-stopping face and the little pointed ears sticking up on either side of her black wool beanie, midnight hair spilling in a tangle of curls down her back. But this is the real thing. The difference between her and the animé Diesel I've been drawing is as profound as it would be between you and the caricature someone might draw of you.

"You're getting it all wrong," she says.

"I think I need a time-out," I tell her.

"That's what the other big-head said."

"Big head? I don't have a big head."

"Oh, relax. It's just what we call you."

"I just think if you're going to insult somebody, you should at least be accurate."

I can't believe I'm arguing with an eight-inch tall oil fairy about the size of my head.

She stands up, puts a hand on her hip and glares at me. I've drawn her in that exact same pose, only much more cartoony.

"Oh, but you can write whatever you want about *us,*" she says. "I can't believe how you're telling the story. I'm goofing with Crude just to get Slick to give me some space."

"But—"

"He's always just so *there*. Sometimes I feel like I can't even breathe."

"I didn't even know you were real," I say. I resist the urge to poke at her with a finger. "Are you real?"

"Of course I'm real."

"And you live in a refinery?"

"Where else would a refinery fairy live?"

She's got me there.

"So where is your refinery?" I ask.

She gives an exaggerated sigh. "Don't you read what you write? It's 'east of wherever, on the far side of dreams.' Like it says on page one."

I lean back in my chair.

"This is going to take some getting used to," I tell her.

"Oh, please. Like you're not dating a werewolf."

"He's not a werewolf, he's a—"

"Canid. I know. A shapechanger. Same difference. He still turns into a wolf."

Though not for me. If I hadn't seen his face…*shift* that one time, when the other shapechangers were ready to attack us, I don't know what I'd believe. I asked him once why he doesn't change in front of me and he said he didn't want me to start thinking of him as my pet dog. I'm not a hundred percent sure he was joking.

"So are you going to fix it?" Diesel asks.

"Fix what?"

For a moment I think she's talking about my relationship with Lyle and there's nothing to fix. At least not on his part. I'm the one with confusion banging around in my head.

"The story," she says. "What else?"

"What did Nina say?" I ask, hoping to buy myself a little time.

"She said I should talk to you."

I'm paying attention to our conversation, really I am, but at the same time I'm so fascinated to see her standing here, this real flesh-and-blood version of something I thought Nina and I had made up. She's got the poutiest lips and that figure. No wonder half the guys in Refinerytown are so crazy about her.

"Hello, big-head?" Diesel says. "Are you still with me?"

I blink. "My name's Mona," I tell her.

"I know that."

"How can you *be* here?" I ask. "I mean—"

"As in, you and your friend made us up, how can we be real, blah blah blah."

"Well...yeah."

She gives me this wicked little grin, which is *just* the way I've drawn her when she's about to say something dazzlingly obvious to Slick or Dipstick.

"Magic," she says.

"Well, if that's not a cop-out, then I don't know what is."

"Look," she says. "The hows and whys of it aren't really important. What's important is that if you're going to tell our story, you have to tell it right."

"You'll help?"

"Well, duh. How else are you going to fix it?"

"Can I take a one-day rain check on...what? Interviewing you?"

"Take as long as you want," she says. "Just don't draw any more lies."

"How will I reach you?" I ask.

She gives me that grin again, but this time it's the version that says, I know a secret that you don't.

"Just call my name."

"But how will you hear me all the way over in Refinerytown?"

"What makes you think we're ever any further than a thought away?"

And then, *phwisht,* she's gone.

I think about what she just said. Great. Another invisible presence in my life. That cranky dwarf who did the home-invasion thing a few years ago and moved in on me? He could do the invisible thing, too. It's just creepy.

"I don't like being spied on," I tell the air where she was standing.

"Welcome to the club," her husky, disembodied voice replies.

"I just had the weirdest conversation," I say when Nina picks up the phone at her end.

"With an eight-inch-tall oil fairy?"

"Bingo."

"I should have called," she says, "but to tell you the truth, I thought I was having an incident."

"What do you mean?"

"Seeing things, like this friend of mine does when he forgets to take his medication."

"What are you taking medication for?" I ask.

My amazement at what I've just experienced flees in the face of worry for her.

"Nothing," she assures me. "It was just an analogy."

"A writer thing."

"A writer thing," she agrees. "You know, big words, hidden meanings. All the deep stuff."

She can always make me laugh.

"So what do you think we should do?" I ask.

Nina doesn't even pause to think.

"Tell their story," she says.

"But what if they all start showing up to tell their part?"

Nina laughs. "Well, then you'll have a whole life-sized contingent of models, ready and willing to pose for you. Weren't you telling me that you were having a little trouble with the action scenes?"

I wait a beat, then say. "Remember your story about the snake who wants wings? What was his name again?"

"Pelican Bob."

"Right. You're on your own with that one."

Jilly's by herself when I go over to the professor's house the next day. I come around the back as usual to the greenhouse door and see her through the window. She's sitting in her wheelchair with a laptop computer on the low worktable in front of her. She's got some kind of pen in her hand that she's using on what looks like a fancy mouse pad. When I tap on the glass, she waves me in.

"Hey, you," she says.

"Hey, yourself. What're you doing?"

She gets this cute little proud smile. "Have a look," she says.

When I come stand behind her shoulder, I see that she's using a pen and tablet to input information into the laptop. There's a drawing program window open on the screen showing an incredibly intricate piece of art. Fairies like she used to paint, hovering around an old coffee tin in what looks like an empty lot.

I know she can't draw or paint anymore. I also know that all her fairy paintings were destroyed after the accident. So while this piece is in her style, it can't be hers.

"Very nice," I say. "Where'd it come from?"

"Me," she says.

My gaze drops down to where the hand of her bad arm lies limply on her lap.

"But…"

She laughs. "No, I haven't gone all dotty on you. It takes me forever, but I can actually do art again with this program."

"I don't understand. You still have to be able to draw to input the lines."

She nods. "Yes, but you can do it as small as a pixel at a time if you want. So even if I can't get the expression I once could in my lines, I can get the detail again. Here, look."

She shows me how she magnifies a small section of the drawing and then adds some pixels with the pen on the tablet. When she reduces the image again, the fairy to the right of the coffee tin has a little more shading under her eyes.

"This is so cool," I tell her. "How long have you been working like this?"

"It feels like forever. This is only my first one and I started it over a month ago."

"And never told a soul."

She shakes her head. "Except for Sophie. I guess I just wanted to make sure I could actually do it."

"How does it feel—working on a screen like that instead of on paper or canvas?"

"Kind of distancing. I really miss the hands-on part of the process."

I have to smile. Jilly hasn't had paint on her hands or in her hair for over a year. It used to be like jewelry—there was always a speck here, a drop there. Vivid colours creating sudden happy highlights. Sometimes I've wanted to splash some on her, just for old time's sake.

"But at least I can do it again," she adds.

She does something on the tablet and a little window pops up asking her if she wants to save her work. She clicks "save" and then shuts down the computer.

"Sophie left me some tea in the thermos," she says. "I'm sure there's enough for both of us. Do you want some?"

"Sure. Let me—"

But she's already wheeling over to the sink. She reaches for a pair of cups and the thermos, then comes back with them on her lap to where I'm sitting.

"You'd better do the honours," she says, handing me the thermos. "I can do it, but the tea'd probably be cold by the time I'm done."

I pour us both a cup, then close the thermos and set it on the table beside the laptop.

"Is that the professor's?" I ask, nodding at the machine.

"No, it's Goon's. He says he never uses it."

"Grumpy Goon actually lent you his laptop?"

"I know. Go figure." She takes a sip of her tea. "So what brings you down out of your studio? Not that I'm complaining. I'm happy for the company. But I thought you had a deadline."

"I do," I tell her. "It's just that I met Diesel last night."

There's a long pause as she registers that.

"Diesel as in the refinery fairy from your comic?" she finally asks.

"The same. In the flesh. The very tiny flesh. She really is only eight inches tall."

Jilly leans forward, a happy smile curving her lips.

"I think you need to tell me everything," she says.

So I do. I mean if you can't tell Jilly about something like this, then who can you tell?

"She came back again after I got off the phone with Nina," I say, finishing up, "and we talked some more about how she thinks the story should go. But I don't know. I told her I'd have to think about it."

"Because it feels like everything's being pulled out of your hands?"

"Pretty much. I mean, I was expecting to collaborate with Nina. But this…it's so weird having the characters tell you what the story should be."

Jilly smiles.

"I tried to convince her to come visit you with me, but she said, and I quote, 'It's not to be.'"

Jilly nods. "I'm not surprised. Fairy visitations are usually very personal. It's in their nature to be secretive."

"But I really wanted you to see her."

"I will. The way everyone will be able to: in your story."

"It's not my story anymore. It's hers. Theirs."

"But isn't that what you wanted?" Jilly asks. "To get away from yourself a little?"

"I suppose I did."

"And besides. This is the way stories are supposed to be. True to themselves—not to how we want them to be."

"Like life, I guess."

Jilly shakes her head. "In life we have to be true to ourselves."

I nod. Jilly's always had this way of stating the obvious so that it feels like a revelation.

"How do you keep the pieces of your life separate from each other?" I ask her.

"What makes you think I do?"

I shrug. "I don't know. You always seem so centered. Even with all that's happened to you."

She looks out of a window for a long moment, gaze focused on something other than the professor's gardens and lawn. Finally she turns to me again.

"Things don't always work out the way we want them to," she says. "I know that, big-time. Not when I was a kid. Not when that car ran me down. So I guess I've learned to make a point of taking charge of whatever parts of my life I *can* control. And really appreciating the aspects that are good. It's like how things are going with Daniel and me."

Daniel's her current beau, this drop-dead gorgeous nurse she met when she was in the ICU, right after the accident.

"I could worry about what he sees in me," she goes on. "You know, he's this active, handsome guy and here's me, the Broken Girl. And I did, at first. But he doesn't see any limitations in our relationship, so why should I go looking for them?"

"So you think I should tell Diesel's story."

She shakes her head. "I think you should do whatever your heart tells you is the right thing to do."

And that, I realize, could as easily apply to every part of my life, not just my refinery fairies comic. If you follow your heart, maybe you don't have to be confused.

---

"Diesel," I say.

I'm sitting alone in my apartment that night, at the drawing table, a pad of plain paper in front of me, a pencil in my hand. I expect her to immediately pop into sight out of nowhere but it's actually a few moments before she does. She notices the miniature armchair that I've left for her at the top of my drawing table and smiles. I bought it at a toy store on the way home from Jilly's.

"Very nice," she says as she falls into it, lounging with her legs over one arm with the instant ease of a cat.

I lift the pencil I'm holding. "I'm ready to do it your way."

She swings her feet to the table and leans forward to look at me, elbows on her knees, hands propping her head. I'm hardly aware of my own hand bringing the pencil to the paper to capture the pose. She grins and starts to talk.

"Wait a minute," I say when we're five minutes into this convoluted story about the various relationships between herself and the other fairies. "We only have thirty-two pages."

"What do you mean?"

"We can't tell your whole life story in this comic. We have to focus on just one aspect of it, the way I do with my strips."

"But it's all important."

I think about the way I worry when I'm pasting and editing the portions of my life that show up in the strips.

"I know," I tell her. "But we have to work within our space limitations. Maybe if this one does well we can do another, but for now we have to be a little more practical about what we use and what we leave out."

"I don't know how to make a lifetime smaller."

I get this sense that she's about to get up and walk off with that swagger she has, stepping away into nothing and I'll never see her again.

"You don't have to," I tell her. "That's my job—to pick what we use. Why don't you just tell it to me the way you need to tell it and I'll take what I think will fit into a thirty-two page story. If you can trust me to do it right."

She gives me a long, considering look, then finally nods.

"Of course I trust you," she says. "And if you get it wrong, I can always turn you into a salamander."

"You can do that?"

She just winks.

"Let me tell you how I first met Slick," she says.

Nina and I have been back-and-forthing faxes of notes and rough storyboards, trying to find a way to tell the story in the pages we have without making it seem either rushed or too cram-packed with detail. There are so many things that are killing us to leave out.

Tonight we're on the phone again, both of us with pages spread out in front of us.

"So did we make them up," I say at one point, "or were they always there and we just somehow tuned into them when we started this thing."

Nina laughs. "Does it matter?"

I suppose maybe it doesn't. How very Zen of us.

Later I'm on the phone with Lyle. He tells me he's been trying to get through all night, but he's just saying it. He doesn't sound impatient or annoyed or anything.

We've been having a moony conversation, the kind you have when you haven't seen each other for awhile and the missing part is really kicking in. Somehow we get onto his shapechanging.

"What's so wrong with you being my pet dog?" I say. "I'll be your pet Boho girl. We can take turns being pets. Pets have it good, you know. Lots of pampering and treats and tickles behind the ear."

He laughs. "What are you really trying to say here, Mona?"

I surprise myself probably as much as him.

"I think we should live together," I say. "That way our differences will get to know each other better and I won't have this constant confusion following me about. What do you think?"

It kind of comes out all in one breath and then there's this long silence on the other end of the line. My heart goes very still. If my friend Sue were here she'd be shaking her finger at me, telling me something about how girls aren't supposed to be assertive, it just scares guys away. She's really sweet, but she does have some old-fashioned ideas.

But maybe I *have* blown it.

What do *I* know about relationships? It's not like I ever had one that really worked before.

I'm about to say something about how I was just kidding when I swear that I can actually feel his smile coming across the phone lines to me.

"I think I'd like that very much," he says.

Okay. So the confusion didn't really go away. I think maybe it never does. When things become clear in one part of your life, I guess your capacity for confusion just attaches itself to another part. But I'm learning not to focus so much on it, to worry about what this means, or that means. I'm trying to take things at face value instead.

The comic's almost done, though I swear Diesel could try the patience of a saint. I'm starting to have some real sympathy for Slick. Diesel and I argue so much, there are times when I feel like she's really going to turn me into a salamander. Lyle says he'll love me anyway, but I don't know. I think a salamander is really pushing it.

You want to know the funniest thing? Nina has me half-convinced to do that Pelican Bob story with her when we're done with this one. Remember him? The little snake who wanted wings?

*AUTHOR'S NOTE:*

With "Refinerytown" I've gone and broken a long-held rule for my writing and put a couple of real people in the story as actual characters. Sharyn November is my editor at Viking, a magnificent woman who really does have chicken puppets, though I've yet to see them. Nina Hoffman is my good pal, a wonderful writer, a talented musician, and a fellow lover of silly things and toys.

They're here because "Refinerytown" started as a joke at a convention. We kept trying to convince Sharyn to buy the idea as a series of picture books, and the more serious we appeared to be, the more horrified she became. There were others involved in the creation of "Refinerytown," most prominently Charles Vess. He didn't make it in because the story already has a comic book artist in it, but he does get a mention. I don't even get that.

And you can blame MaryAnn for telling me I should actually write the story. I think she meant the *real* "Refinerytown," but I'm leaving that in Mona's and Nina's capable hands.

# *A Crow Girls'*
# *Christmas*

"We have jobs," Maida told Jilly when she and Zia dropped by the professor's house for a visit at the end of November.

Zia nodded happily. "Yes, we've become veryvery respectable."

Jilly had to laugh. "I can't imagine either of you ever being completely respectable."

That comment drew an exaggerated pout from each of the crow girls, the one more pronounced than the other.

"Not being completely respectable's a good thing," Jilly assured them.

"Yes, well, easy for you to say," Zia said. "You don't have a cranky uncle always asking when you're going to do something useful for a change."

Maida nodded. "You just get to wheel around and around in your chair and not worry about all the very serious things that we do."

"Such as?" Jilly asked.

Zia shrugged. "Why *don't* pigs fly?"

"Or why is white a colour?" Maida offered.

"Or black."

"Or yellow ochre."

"Yellow ochre is a colour," Jilly said. "Two colours, actually. And white and black are colours, too. Though I suppose they're not very *colourful,* are they?"

"Could it be more puzzling?" Zia asked.

Maida simply smiled and held out her tea cup. "May I have a refill, please?"

Jilly pushed the sugar bag over to her. Maida filled her tea cup to the brim with sugar. After a glance at Zia, she filled Zia's tea cup as well.

"Would you like some?" she asked Jilly.

"No, I'm quite full. Besides, too much tea makes me have to pee."

The crow girls giggled.

"So what sort of jobs did you get?" Jilly asked.

Zia lowered her tea cup and licked the sugar from her upper lip.

"We're elves!" she said.

Maida nodded happily. "At the mall. We get to help out Santa."

"Not the real Santa," Zia explained.

"No, no. He's much too very busy making toys at the North Pole."

"This is sort of a cloned Santa."

"Every mall has one, you know."

"And we," Zia announced proudly, "are in charge of handing out the candy canes."

"Oh my," Jilly said, thinking of the havoc that could cause.

"Which makes us very important," Maida said.

"Not to mention useful."

"So pooh to Lucius, who thinks we're not."

"Do they have lots of candy canes in stock?" Jilly asked.

"Mountains," Zia assured her.

"Besides," Maida added. "It's all magic, isn't it? Santa never runs out of candy or toys."

That was before you were put in charge of the candy canes, Jilly thought, but she kept her worry to herself.

Much to everyone's surprise, the crow girls made excellent elves. They began their first daily four-hour shift on December 1st, dressed in matching red and green outfits that the mall provided: long-sleeved jerseys, short pleated skirts, tights, shoes with exaggerated curling toes, and droopy elf hats with their rowdy black hair poking out from underneath. There were bells on their shoes, bells at the end of their hats, and they each wore brooches made of bells that they'd borrowed from one of the stores in the mall. Because they found it next to impossible to stand still for more than a few seconds at a time, the area around Santa's chair echoed with their constant jingling. Parents waiting in line, not to mention their eager children, were completely enchanted by their happy antics and the ready smiles on their small dark faces.

"I thought they'd last fifteen minutes," their uncle Lucius confided to the professor a few days after the pair had started, "but they've surprised me."

"I don't see why," the professor said. "It seems to me that they'd be perfectly suited for the job. They're about as elfish as you can get without being an elf."

"But they're normally so easily distracted."

The professor nodded. "However, there's candy involved, isn't there? Jilly tells me that they've put in charge of the candy canes."

"And isn't that a source for pride." Lucius shook his head and smiled. "Trust them to find a way to combine sweets with work."

"They'll be the Easter Bunny's helpers in the spring."

Lucius laughed. "Maybe I can apprentice them to the Tooth Fairy."

The crow girls really were perfectly suited to their job. Unlike many of the tired shoppers that trudged by Santa's chair, they remained enthralled with every aspect of their new environment. The flashing lights. The jingling bells. The glittering tinsel. The piped-in Christmas music. The shining ornaments.

And, of course, the great abundance of candy canes.

They treated each child's questions and excitement as though that child was the first to have this experience. They talked to those waiting in line, made faces so that the children would laugh happily as they were having their pictures taken, handed out candy canes when the children were lifted down from Santa's lap. They paid rapt attention to every wish expressed and adored hearing about all the wonderful toys available in the shops.

Some children, normally shy about a visit to Santa, returned again and again, completely smitten with the pair.

But mostly, it was all about the candy canes.

The crow girls were extremely generous in handing them out, and equally enthusiastic about their own consumption. They stopped themselves from eating as many as they might have liked, but did consume one little candy cane each for every five minutes they were on the job.

Santa, busy with the children, and also enamored with his cheerful helpers, failed to notice that the sacks of candy canes in the storage area behind his chair were dwindling at an astonishing rate. He never thought to look because it had never been an issue before. There'd always been plenty of candy canes to go around in the past.

On December 19th, at the beginning of their noon shift, there were already lines and lines of children waiting excitedly to visit Santa and his crow girl elves. As the photographer was unhooking the cord to let the children in, Maida turned to Zia to ask where the next sack of candy canes was just as Zia asked Maida the very same question. Santa suggested that they'd better hurry up and grab another sack from the storage space.

Trailing the sound of jingling bells, the crow girls went behind his chair.

Zia pulled aside the little curtain.

"Oh-oh," she said.

Maida pushed in beside her to have a look herself. The two girls exchanged worried looks.

"They're all gone," Zia told Santa.

"I'll go to the stockroom for more," Maida offered.

Zia nodded. "Me, too."

"What stockroom?" Santa began.

But then he realized exactly what they were saying. His normally rosy cheeks went as white as his whiskers.

"They're all gone?" he asked. *"All* those bags of candy canes?"

"In a word, yes."

"But where could they all have gone?"

"We gave them away," Maida reminded him. "Remember?"

Zia nodded. "We were supposed to."

"So that's what we did."

"Because it's our job."

"And we ate a few," Maida admitted.

"A veryvery few."

Santa frowned. "How many is a few?"

"Hmm," Zia said.

"Good question."

"Let's see."

They both began to count on their fingers as they talked.

"We were veryvery careful not to eat more than twelve an hour."

"Oh so very careful."

"So in four hours—"

"—that would be forty-eight—"

"—times two—"

"—because there are two of us."

They paused for a moment, as though to ascertain that there really were only two of them.

"So that would be...um..."

"Ninety-six—"

"—times how many days?"

"Eighteen—"

"—not counting today—"

"—because there aren't any today—"

"—which is why we need to go the stockroom to get more."

Santa was adding it all up himself. "That's almost two thousand candy canes you've eaten!"

"Well, almost," Maida said.

"One thousand, seven hundred and twenty-eight," Zia said.

"If you're keeping count."

"Which is *almost* two thousand, I suppose, but not really."

"Where is the candy cane stockroom?" Maida asked.

"There isn't one," Santa told her.

"But—"

"And that means," he added, "that all the children here today won't get any candy canes."

The crow girls looked horrified.

"That means us, too," Zia said.

Maida nodded. "We'll also suffer, you know."

"But we're ever so stoic."

"Ask anybody."

"We'll hardly complain."

"And never where you can hear us."

"Except for now, of course."

Santa buried his face in hands, completely disconcerting the parent approaching his chair, child in hand.

"Don't worry!" Maida cried.

"We have everything under control." Zia looked at Maida. "We do, don't we?"

Maida closed her eyes for a long moment, then opened them wide and grinned.

"Free tinsel for everyone!" she cried.

"I don't want tinsel," the little boy standing in front of Santa with his mother said. "I want a candy cane."

"Oh, you do want tinsel," Maida assured him.

"Why does he want tinsel?" Zia asked.

"Because...because..."

Maida grabbed two handfuls from the boughs of Santa's Christmas tree. Fluttering the tinsel with both hands over her head, she ran around the small enclosure that housed Santa's chair.

"Because it's so fluttery!" she cried.

Zia immediately understood. "And shiny!" Grinning, she grabbed handfuls of her own.

"Veryvery shiny," Maida agreed.

"And almost as good as candy," Zia assured the little boy as she handed him some. "Though not quite as sugary good."

The little boy took the tinsel with a doubtful look, but then Zia whirled him about in a sudden impromptu dance. Soon he was laughing and waving his tinsel as well. From the line-up, all the children began to clap.

"We want tinsel, too!" one of them cried.

"Tinsel, tinsel!"

The crow girls got through their shift with great success. They danced and twirled on the spot and did mad acrobatics. They fluttered tinsel, blew kisses, jingled their bells, and told stories so outrageous that no one believed them, but everyone laughed.

By the end of their shift, even Santa had come around to seeing "the great excellent especially good fortune of free tinsel."

Unfortunately, the mall management wasn't so easily appeased and the crow girls left the employ of the Williamson Street Mall that very day, after first having to turn in their red and green elf outfits. But on the plus side, they were paid for their nineteen days of work and spent all their money on chocolate and fudge and candy and ice cream.

When they finally toddled out of the mall into the snowy night, they made chubby snow angels on any lawn they could find, all the way back to the Rookery.

"So now we're unemployed," Zia told Jilly when they came over for a visit on the twenty-third, shouting "Happy eve before Christmas eve!" as they trooped into the professor's house.

"I heard," Jilly said.

"It was awful," Maida said.

Jilly nodded. "Losing a job's never fun."

"No, no, no," Zia said. "They ran out of candy canes!"

"Can you imagine?" Maida asked.

Zia shook her head. "Barely. And I was there."

"Well, I'm sorry to hear that," Jilly said.

"Yes, it's a veryvery sorrysome state of affairs," Maida said.

"And we're unemployed, too!"

"Lucius says we're unemployable."

"Because now we have a record."

"A permanent record."

"Of being bad bad candy cane-eating girls."

They both looked so serious and sad that Jilly became worried. But then Zia laughed. And Maida laughed, too.

"What's so funny?" Jilly asked.

Zia started to answer, but she collapsed in giggles and couldn't speak.

Maida giggled, too, but she managed to say, "We sort of like being bad bad candy cane-eating girls."

Zia got her fit of giggles under control. "Because it's like being outlaws."

"Fierce candy cane-eating outlaw girls."

"And that's a good thing?" Jilly asked.

"What do you think?" Maida asked.

"I think it is. Merry Christmas, Maida. Merry Christmas, Zia."

"Merry Christmas to you!" they both cried.

Zia looked at Maida. "Why did you say, 'Merry Christmas toot toot'?"

"I didn't say 'toot toot'."

"I think maybe you did."

"Didn't."

Zia grinned. "Toot toot!"

"Toot toot!"

They pulled their jingling bell brooches out of their pockets which they'd forgotten to return to the store where they'd "found" them and marched around the kitchen singing "Jingle Bells" at the top of their lungs until Goon, the professor's housekeeper, came in and made them stop.

Then they sat at the table with their cups of sugar, on their best behavior which meant they only took their brooches out every few moments, jingled them and said "toot toot" very quietly. Then giggling, they'd put the brooches away again.

# Sweet Forget-Me-Not

"**Y**ou don't want to get involved with the likes of them."

I turned to see who'd spoken, feeling a little nervous because I was skipping school, but it was only Ernie, the old guy who did odd jobs around the neighbourhood. He had a little apartment in back of the Seafair Theatre, but I guess he didn't spend much time there because you'd see him out in the streets at all hours of the day and night.

I've heard my parents tut-tutting about him, the way lots of people in the neighbourhood do. Everybody seems to think it's a shame that a person can live their life the way he does, day to day, with no ambition. But I don't see a lack of ambition as that bad a personality trait. I mean, what if you don't have this drive to succeed at something? Are you supposed to pretend you do, just to fit in?

My parents would say yes. That's if they could even understand the question.

"Involved with who?" I asked.

I could hear my mom correcting my grammar in my head. Being an immigrant, she was very particular about how we use the language of her adopted country. I know she means well, but it gets old.

"Don't play the fool with me, boy," Ernie said. "I'm talking about that gaggle of girls you've been staring at for the last ten minutes."

"You can see them?"

"Do I look blind?"

I shook my head. "But nobody else seems to notice them."

"That's because most people *are* blind."

They'd have to be.

It was the colour of them that first attracted my attention, and I don't just mean their clothing or their race. There seemed to be around six of them, but I kept losing count. Their hair was a wild tangle of curls ranging in colour from a rich mauve to shocking pinks. The ones with loose pants had tight tops, the ones with baggy shirts wore tights under them, and they all had clunky shoes that didn't seem to cause them the least bit of a problem as they danced and pirouetted about, as light on their feet as acrobats or ballerinas. The colour of their clothes was as wild as their hair—bright yellows, reds, pinks and greens—and there wasn't much to them. They were just a gang of tall, skinny girls with narrow features and the same Mediterranean cast to their skin that I have.

"So what are they doing?" I asked as we watched them dance about.

They were singing something, too, but I couldn't make out the words. I could tell it had a beat, though. A little hip hop, a little rhyming set to a finger-snapping beat.

"What do you think?" Ernie said. "They're having fun."

"I thought maybe they were stoned."

He laughed. "They don't need stimulants to have fun."

Well, they looked totally blissed-out to me, but what did I know? I still couldn't figure out how they could be having such a grand time, dancing and goofing around the way they were—and the way they looked—but nobody seemed to notice. I know people get jaded, but you'd think *somebody* would turn and have a look as they walked by the alley where the girls were having their fun, if only to shake their heads and then go on.

But there was only me, turned the wrong way around on a bus stop bench and getting a crick in my neck. And now Ernie.

"Why did you say I shouldn't get involved with them?" I asked.

"Because they only stay around long enough to break your heart."

"What's that supposed to mean?"

"They're gemmin," Ernie said. "Little mobile histories of a place. Kind of like fairies, if you think of them as the spirits of a place."

"Yeah, right."

He shrugged. "You asked, so I'm telling you."

"Fairies."

"Except they're called gemmin. They soak up stories and memories, and then one day they're all full up and off they go."

I couldn't believe this stupid story of his, but I couldn't help wanting to know more at the same time. Because there was the plain fact that *no one* seemed to notice them but us.

"So where do they go?" I asked.

"I don't know. I just know they go and they don't come back. Not the same ones, anyway."

I gave him a look. "What's that supposed to mean?"

"You're pretty full of questions, boy. Don't you have someplace better to be, like school?"

"I don't like school."

"Yeah, well, I'm with you on that." He shakes his head. "When I think of all the crap they expect you to remember—like it's ever going to be any use unless you become a brain surgeon or an accountant."

"No, I don't mind learning," I said. "I kind of like that part of it."

"Sure," he said. "If it's something you *want* to learn, right? But you can get that out of a library."

I shook my head. "No, I find it all pretty interesting."

He shook his head like he thought *I* was the one who was weird. He's not alone. Can you say nerd? That's me.

"Then what's the problem?" he asked.

"I just don't…you know, get along with the other kids much."

He nodded. "You telling them stuff they don't want to hear?"

"It's more like them telling me."

He'd been standing beside me on the sidewalk, but now he took a seat on the bench.

"What's your name?" he asked.

"Ahmad Nasrallah."

"Well, what are they ragging you about? You look like a nice, normal kid."

"No, I look like a terrorist."

He studied me for a long moment, then gave me another nod, a slow one this time.

"Because of the colour of your skin," he said.

"Yeah. And my name. But my family's not from Afghanistan or Iraq or whatever. We're Lebanese. We're not even Muslims—although I guess my parents were before they immigrated. But I was born right here in this city."

"There's nothing wrong being Muslim," Ernie said. "There's bad apples in whatever way you want to group people—doesn't matter if it's religious, political, or social. The big mistake is generalizing."

"Doesn't stop them from doing it."

"Yeah, people are like that." He smiled. "And there's another generalization for you."

"So did you have trouble in school, too?" I asked.

"Oh, yeah. I was like a trouble magnet. And opening my mouth didn't help much either."

"So that's what you meant when you asked if I was telling people things they don't want to hear."

He nodded. "I had me a big mouth, no question. But the real problem was I couldn't stop talking about…them."

He didn't look at the gemmin, but I knew who he meant.

I couldn't imagine telling anybody at school about them. Why would I give the kids more ammunition?

"Why'd you do it?" I asked. "You had to know they'd make fun of you."

He shrugged. "It started in grade school, when I didn't know any better and the teasing just followed me through the years—long after I'd stopped talking about it. But the thing is, if anybody asked me straight out, I couldn't lie. Not because of who was asking, but because I thought lying would diminish the gemmin." He gave me a sad smile. "Like in *Peter Pan,* you know?"

I shook my head.

"Every time a kid says they don't believe in fairies, another one of them dies."

"Is that true?"

"I don't think so now. But it seemed possible back then. I didn't realize that they weren't dying. It's hard to see from here, but their eyes are the most amazing sapphire blue that turn to violet as they get filled up with the little histories around them. And once they do fill up, they leave."

I thought about that, then asked, "What did you mean about the same ones not coming back? Who does come back?"

"Coming back's not exactly the right way to describe it. You see those bits of colour that seemed to spin off them sometimes, when they're dancing really hard?"

I nodded. "I thought they were ribbons or confetti or something."

"I don't know what they are either. But if you watch one long enough, you'll see it kind of disappears into the ground. I don't know what happens underground, out of our sight, but something does. Either a piece of that colour incubates down there, or a bunch of them gather together, but eventually, when the ones we're looking at are gone, some new gemmin will come sprouting up."

He smiled, a far away look in his eyes.

"They're just like the fairies I remember in the stories I read as a kid," he went on after a moment. "When they're new, I mean. Tiny, perfect little creatures."

"And then they grow up to be like these?"

The ones we were looking at seemed to be in their early to mid-teens, around my age, which was still fifteen. I wouldn't turn sixteen until next month. Unlike a lot of the girls in school who were already all curves and breasts, the gemmin were skinny, flat-chested and almost hipless. They could almost be boys, except you knew from their faces that they were girls. And though they didn't have a lot of shape to them, they were still hot, like you'd see in some magazine.

I imagined kissing one of them and felt my neck and face get warm.

"They're really...sexy, aren't they?" I found myself saying.

Ernie laughed. "Not to me. I just see a bunch of cute kids. But I remember I felt different when I was your age."

"You're not that old."

But then I had to wonder how old he was. I figured he had to be at least forty, which was older than I could ever imagine being. Your life'd pretty much be over by then. I just had to look at my parents and their friends. They never seemed to have any fun, except every once in awhile at a wedding or something, when they'd get a little goofy after having too much wine.

"I'm old enough to be their father," Ernie said. He said it in a certain tone of voice that made me think, for a moment, that he was going to rub my head, the way Uncle Joe does. "I don't rob cradles, Ahmad."

Whatever.

"So do they live here?" I asked. "In this alley?"

Ernie shook his head. "You'll see them all over the city—different little groups of them—but this bunch usually comes back here. They seem to have laid claim to our neighbourhood, and that Dodge in particular."

He was talking about the junked stationwagon that had been abandoned at the back of the alley. You see useless cars like that all the time around this part of town. They'll be in an empty lot or behind some building for a few months, slowly getting stripped of useable parts. Eventually somebody in one of the neighbouring buildings gets the city to have it towed away.

"I've lived here all my life," I said, "so how come I've never seen them before?"

"Maybe you never really needed to."

"What's that supposed to mean?"

He shrugged. "How were you feeling when you first sat down on this bench?"

"I was fine."

"No, really. You told me you were skipping school. That the kids there had been ragging on you."

"Okay. So maybe I was a little pissed off."

"And sad? Or at least feeling hurt?"

"Yeah, whatever."

I didn't know where this was going, but it was making me uncomfortable to talk about it.

"And how do you feel now?" he asked.

"I told you, I feel fine."

"Maybe even a little happy?"

Then I realized what he was getting at. If I was going to be honest, I felt a lot better now than when I'd first gotten here. Before I'd noticed the gemmin and sat down, I'd been fantasizing about how I could get back at Joey Draves and the Ross brothers—the ones that were riding me the hardest. They weren't alone, but the other kids that gave me a rough time were just echoing Joey and his gang. Trying to show how they were cool, too. It didn't seem to help them much, but they didn't stop either. The only way it'd ever stop was if Joey and the Ross brothers laid off, and that wasn't going to happen any time soon. It was like I'd become a pet project for them.

But the funny thing was, while the fantasy of getting back at them was still a going concern—sitting there somewhere in my head where the stuff you can't get away from does—right now I couldn't really muster up a whole lot of anger towards them.

"Yeah, I guess," I told Ernie. I wasn't looking at him as I spoke, but at the gemmin. It was hard not to look at them. "I feel pretty good, actually."

"I've noticed that over the years," Ernie said. "The people who do seem to become aware of them are the ones that need a little help with the load they're carrying. It doesn't seem to work for everybody who's feeling bad. I've seen depressed people walk right through a crowd of gemmin and never notice them. But when people do, it's usually when they're feeling low."

"And then they start feeling better," I said. "Like magic."

Ernie laughed. "Hell, they *are* magic. But it's not some kind of cureall. It's more like they give you a respite. A bit of time to regroup and take stock of the big picture, you know?"

I looked at him and shook my head.

"No matter how good a reason a person's got for feeling bad," he said, "a change of perspective is sometimes all you need to get back on track again."

"And that's what they're for?" I asked.

He laughed again. "Not likely. I think the feeling good part is just a side effect of being around them. You know, you take in the pure joy that they seem to find in life and you can't help but feeling a little better yourself. But they're not here for us. They just are."

"They're something, all right."

"So sometimes," Ernie went on, "when I run across a person who seems to be feeling pretty down, I try to steer them to wherever the nearest gemmin are hanging out—just in case it can help, you know?"

So he did have an ambition—it was just a weird and useless one that you couldn't talk to anyone about, except another loser like me.

"How'd you figure out all of this stuff?" I asked.

"They told me."

I turned to look at the gemmin, still fooling around in the alley. Singing and dancing. I wondered what they'd tell me if I could get up the nerve to talk to them.

"They like meeting people," Ernie said, as though he was reading my mind. Maybe he was just reading my face. "They like making friends. The trouble is—"

I remembered what he'd said before, and finished it for him: "They end up breaking your heart."

"That pretty much sums it up."

There was a look in his eyes that I'd never seen before and I knew that when he talked about a broken heart it had nothing to do with what you hear in the songs on the Top 40. It wasn't even like when Sandy Lohnes broke up with me last spring because she didn't want to be going steady with somebody whose relatives were probably all terrorists. It wasn't anything she ever said, and I didn't think she actually believed it herself, but we both knew that was the reason all the same. It was what people were saying to her—the black cloud hanging over me starting to include her as well.

I carried a lot of anger around when she dumped me. Sadness, too, but it was nothing like what I saw in Ernie's eyes.

"I think I have to go talk to them anyway," I said.

Ernie nodded. "Yeah. I figured as much."

I wanted to explain it to him, but he got up then and gave me a little salute, first finger tipping away from his brow, and headed off down the sidewalk. It was just as well. I wouldn't have been able to find the words anyway.

It took me awhile to get up my nerve, but finally I pushed myself up from the bench. I shoved my hands deep in the pockets of my cargo pants and kind of shuffled over until I could lean up against the wall, close enough to hear what they were singing. Turned out the words weren't in English. Maybe they couldn't speak English and I wasn't about to try Lebanese.

They noticed me, the way girls notice guys on a street corner, or at the mall, sort of not looking at you, but you can tell they're checking you out. They didn't seem to think I was a total loser—I guess they hadn't been talking to Joey Draves—but I was starting to feel like one anyway. They were just so…special. And I'm not, except to my Mom and Dad. And most of the time to my sister—when I wasn't bugging her. Nothing major, just the usual kid brother stuff.

I was trying to think of a way to just do a quick fade away when the one with the brightest pink hair and this big baggy yellow shirt came up and leaned against the wall beside me, mimicking the way I was standing. The others started to giggle and I thought, oh great. It's even going to happen to me here. But then she grinned and took my hands, pulling me over to where the others were still dancing.

I tried to hold back—I'm the definition of two left feet—but she was stronger than she looked.

"Come on," she said. "What are you so scared of?"

Everything, I wanted to tell her.

"I'm not so good," I told her instead. "You know, at dancing and stuff."

"Then I'll have to teach you."

"You don't want to do that."

"But I do. You can see us. That means you could be our friend and we like having friends."

"Yeah, but—"

"And friends have to dance together."

One of the other girls started making this kind of bass-y noise with her mouth, setting a beat. The others kept time with their feet, clunky shoes tapping the pavement. One of them chimed in with a kind of *shouka-shouka* counter rhythm and then the one holding my hands began to sway back and forth.

"Just find the rhythm," she said. "Move your hips. Like this."

She was skinny under that baggy shirt, but she was sexy as all get-out. No way I could do what she was doing—not and look good the way she did. But when I started to shake my head, she slipped behind me and put her hands on my hips, showing me how to find the beat.

"What's your name?" she asked.

Her voice was right in my ear and I could smell her breath. It was sweet and spicy at the same time, nothing like any other girl's I'd ever been this close to before, which so far has only been three. And I never did kiss one of them—I mean, real kissing. We didn't touch tongues.

"I'm Troon," she said when I told her my name.

The other girls chorused strange words that I realized were their names:

"Shivy."

"Mita."

"Omal."

"Neenie."

"Alaween."

And never once lost the music they were making while they did it. Their names became part of the music. I heard my own in there, too, made even more exotic by the sound of their sweet, husky voices.

Troon let go of my hips and came around in front of me again, the others girls circling around as we danced. Or while they danced and I tried.

But I have to admit, while dancing's nothing I'd ever done in public, I'd tried it lots in my bedroom in front of the mirror. Mostly it was just me trying to figure out how not to make too big an ass of myself, just in case I ever got up the nerve to go to a school dance again. But I did it for fun, too. I'd even tried belly dancing.

My sister Suha took it up for awhile because it seemed like an interesting way of doing aerobics with the added bonus of putting her in touch with a part of our cultural heritage. She said. I think it was just a way to put on a sexy show at weddings and stuff, but in a way that our parents couldn't say was improper.

So anyway, I tried a couple of those moves with the gemmin, and sure enough, they all squealed with laughter and I wished I could disappear into a crack in the pavement. But then I realized they were laughing with me, not at me, and they all started trying to shake their tummies like I'd just done.

That afternoon ended up being the best fun I'd ever had. Troon was the one who'd first got me dancing with them, but the one who really seemed to take a shine to me was Neenie. She was a little shorter than the rest, which made her about my five-six, and had the most perfect sky-blue eyes I've ever seen. Her hair was a tangle of tiny mauve braids and she was wearing big red cargo pants and a tight little pinkish top that showed off her belly button.

And when I finally left to go home for supper, she's the one who came up and gave me a kiss.

"You'll come back, won't you?" she asked.

I was still feeling the press of her body against me and the kiss that was tingling on my lips, and I couldn't find my voice. So I just nodded.

Somebody saw me that afternoon, dancing in the alley with the gemmin, except they didn't see the gemmin, only me. Dancing by myself beside a junked out old stationwagon.

I don't know who it was, but Joey got hold of the story and by noon it was all over the school. I guess it made a change from them calling me

"Osama," or—the height of Joey's stupid repartee—"Al Kida," but I didn't feel any better.

We were out in the schoolyard and they were all in a loose circle around me. I just kept trying to walk away, but whatever part of the circle I approached closed tight as soon as I got near it. Then Joey said something about me dancing with some wet dream in my head and I lost it. And I understood what Ernie'd meant about having to tell the truth about the gemmin, because doing otherwise diminished even the idea of them. At least in my head.

I didn't say anything, but I took a swing at Joey. He ducked it easily and gave me a shove that knocked me off my feet. A moment later we were grappling—I was just trying to hold onto him so that he wouldn't be able to hit me—but then we got busted by Mr. Finn and sent to the principal's office.

Once we were there, Mr. Taggart started lecturing us about how they had zero tolerance for violence on school property. I wondered where the zero tolerance was when Joey and his buddies were ragging on me all the time, but I knew there was no point in bringing it up. That's the way it always goes. Guys like Joey always get away with it. Mr. Taggart probably agreed with Joey that I should just go back to Afghanistan even though I'd never even been there before.

To get him to shut up, I told Mr. Taggart that I'd started it.

That got me a three-day suspension and I knew my parents were going to kill me. Though maybe that was the least of my worries, since the last thing Joey said as we were walking down the hall—him on his way to class, me going home to face the music—was, "This isn't over, Osama."

And I knew it wasn't. I guess the best thing about the suspension was that I was going to have three days before he beat the crap out of me— five actually, I realized, since today was a Tuesday. The worst thing was that I got grounded for two weeks. My parents were really disappointed in me and Dad was into a major lecture before Suha spoke up for me.

"You should be proud of him for standing up for himself," she said, not realizing that this time I'd been standing up for the gemmin. "You should hear the things they call us. Ahmad gets it way worse than me."

"What kind of things?" Dad asked.

I saw him deflate as Suha told him about the whole terrorist business that had been dogging us since 9/11 and realized that he'd probably been the brunt of some of that same crap himself. But then he straightened in his chair.

"Is this true?" he asked me.

I shrugged.

"First thing in the morning," he said, "I'm going to have a talk with that principal of yours."

"Dad, no!" Suha and I cried at the same time.

It took us awhile to convince him that talking to the principal would only make things worse, but finally, he nodded his reluctant agreement.

"Still, fighting's not the answer," he told me. "I want you to remember that."

"I will," I said, wondering what he'd have to say when I came back from school on Monday after Joey'd made good his threat.

"So you're still grounded. And no TV for a week. Suha will get your homework and I expect you to study here at home, just as if you were in school."

The studying part wasn't hard. I wasn't lying to Ernie when I told him that I like learning. But it's hard to do it on your own, all day long. The second day of my suspension I went out and sat on the fire escape that we use as a balcony and stared down the alleyway, wishing I could be with the gemmin. But I knew better than to try to sneak off. One of the neighbours would see me and they'd tell my parents and then who knew how long I'd be grounded.

So I sat there on the steps, feeling sorry for myself, when I suddenly heard a bang on the metal steps behind me, like something big had just fallen onto them. I turned, my heart pounding because—don't ask me how he'd get there—I was sure it was Joey. Except it wasn't. It was Neenie. I don't know how she got there either, but the noise I'd heard was her jumping on the fire escape to get my attention.

"You didn't come see us," she said.

"I couldn't."

"But you said you would. I thought you liked me."

"I *do* like you. It's just…"

"Complicated," she finished for me and came to sit on the step me. "That's the trouble with being a people. *Everything's* complicated."

"It's not for you?"

"No, should it be?"

I shook my head. "No, I'm glad it's simple for you. I wish it was simple for me."

"Make it simple."

I smiled. "Easier said than done."

"Then say it at least."

It took me a moment, but then I realized she was asking me to tell her my problems. I remembered what Ernie had said, how the gemmin collected stories, so I thought, why not? She was probably the only person I could tell my troubles to that wouldn't have to feel the weight of them because they didn't touch her life.

When I was done she locked that perfect blue gaze of hers on mine. Then she leaned close and kissed me. Long. Tongue slipping into my mouth. When we came up for air I was feeling flushed and had to hold my legs together so that she wouldn't see the growing bulge in my pants.

Neenie licked her lips. "You taste good," she said.

"You do, too."

She did. All sweet and spicy, like her breath. I guess all the gemmin were like that. Must be their diet.

"I wish you felt better," she added.

Right now I felt like I was in heaven and I told her so.

She laughed. "Were you ever there?"

"No, but it's supposed to be a place where everything's perfect and that's how I feel right now."

"That's good. I feel heaveny, too."

I don't suppose anyone's ever had a stranger girlfriend—except Ernie, I guess. We spent that afternoon together, moving from the fire escape into my room. I played her some CDs, which she liked a lot, humming along and tapping her toes on the floor. I wondered if it was bothering Mrs. Robins downstairs, but she never came up to complain—and trust me, she would have.

So we listened to music and we necked and we talked and then necked some more. The afternoon went by in a blur. It took her awhile to understand the concept of being grounded, but once she did, she promised she'd come back the next day. And she did. It was harder on the weekend because Suha was in and out of the apartment all day and my parents were home, but she snuck into my room at night and we lay on the bed whispering and kissing until we fell asleep. I never had to worry about anyone catching her in there with me in the morning because nobody but me could see her anyway.

Then came Monday and I had to go to school. Dad reminded me about not fighting and I reminded him that I understood. Mom's eyes were a little misty as she sent us off. She didn't know about Joey's threat, but I guess she didn't like the idea of her kids getting treated badly.

It wasn't so bad for Suha—maybe because she was a girl. She wasn't my idea of pretty—I mean, God, she was my sister—but I knew guys were always totally checking her out. And it helped that her boyfriend threatened to beat the crap out of Joey the first time he tried to do his little game on her.

But I didn't have anyone to stand up for me. The few friends I'd had before all of this started were as small or smaller than me. You couldn't miss us. We were the nerd squad that every school has and while we all desperately wanted to be part of the cool crowd, we spent most of our time just trying to not be noticed. It was safer that way.

Joey waited until after school to make good on his threat.

Suha went off to the mall with some friends, so I had to walk home by myself. I was just as glad. There was no way to stop this from happening, so I'd rather she wasn't there when it did. Not just because I didn't want her to see me humiliated, but to keep her safe in case things got out of hand. She did ask me if I wanted company on the way home, but I told her, no.

"I think he's just going to let it slide," I told her, and conveniently didn't mention the dark looks Joey'd been giving me all day. "He didn't even rag me at lunch."

"Okay. If you think you'll be all right."

"I'll be fine."

So I was alone when they herded me into the empty lot behind that strip of thrift stores and junk shops on Grasso Street. People kept saying condos were going up there, but they'd been saying that for years. I sure wished there were condos now, but I don't suppose it would have mattered. They'd just have gotten me in some alley instead.

Joey led the festivities, the way he always did. With him were Jack and Marty Ross. Phil Kluge. A couple of other guys. More than enough to really hurt me.

I'm useless in a fight—just look what happened last week—but I wasn't going to go down without a struggle. It's not that I was feeling brave. I was probably more scared than I've ever been. But I was mad, too.

They started shoving me back and forth between them. I took a swing at Marty, but he just grinned and pushed me away. And then I saw the last thing in the world I wanted to see: the gemmin, giggling and laughing as they approached us from the far side of the lot.

"Go away!" I cried.

"Not likely, Osama," Joey said.

But I wasn't talking to him and his friends. I didn't want the gemmin getting hurt. I didn't want Neenie to see me get beat up. But then I remembered, the gemmin were invisible to most people. So they wouldn't get hurt. They'd just see me humiliated.

Well, they wouldn't see me go down without a fight.

I charged Joey, but he stepped aside and stuck out his foot. And down I went.

"You want to lick my shoe, raghead?" Joey asked.

Before I could get up, they all moved in, ready to kick the crap out of me. But suddenly the gemmin were among them.

The thing I hadn't considered was that just because they were invisible to most people, didn't mean they weren't there. Neenie bent down behind Joey and Mita gave him a shove. Down he went. Troon had a stick in her hand and she whacked it so hard against Phil's knee that the stick broke. Phil went down, too. So did the Ross brothers and the other two guys as Omal and the other girls went after them. And once they were all down, the gemmin kicked them with their clunky shoes. In the side. On the arm and thigh and leg. Hurting them, but not damaging them. Not the way they'd have hurt me.

Shivy and Alaween ran over to me and pulled me to my feet.

"Time to go," Troon said.

And off we went.

That night when Neenie and I sat together on the fire escape, I wondered aloud if my escape was going to make things better or worse. Better would be if they'd all just ignore me and leave me alone. Worse would be if they got me some place where I wasn't about to be rescued and they really went to town.

"They won't bother you," Neenie said. "We told them you were haunted and they had to leave you alone."

"I thought most people couldn't see you."

"They can't. Only the special people like you can do it on your own. But we can be seen if want to be. And we can be heard. We went back and found them in their homes and whispered into their ears." She grinned. "I gave the meanest one a good whack on the back of the head when he wouldn't listen."

"So you guys aren't all fun and dancing," I said.

"Oh, yes, we are."

"But…"

She laughed. "We can be fierce, too."

"Lucky for me."

"No," she said, snuggling closer. "Lucky for me. I can't have my boyfriend too bruised to hold me."

I put my other arm around her and pulled her tightly against me.

"Or his lips to sore to kiss me," she added.

So I showed her that wasn't the case at all.

I guess she was right. I went to school the next day feeling about as nervous as I've ever felt, but Joey and his friends wouldn't even look at me, except when they thought I wouldn't notice, and then I saw something in their faces that I'd only ever seen on the faces of their victims: Fear.

I'd like to say everything was perfect from there on out, but I guess life just doesn't work that way.

October turned into November and it started to get colder, especially at night. I worried about Neenie and the other gemmin, nesting in their junked car at night, but she assured me that the cold didn't bother them.

"Don't be such a worrywart," she told me. "We're not like you, scared of the cold."

But for all the strange way they lived and the fact that they were invisible to the world at large, it was hard to think of them as not like me.

Neenie gave me a potted flower for my birthday—a little blue forget-me-not. I don't know where she got it, at that time of year.

"It's so you'll think of me," she said.

"I'm always thinking about you."

"You're so sweet."

November became December.

Around the middle of the month, Neenie and I were walking up Flood Street after school, when she paused by the Chinese grocery store to eavesdrop on a conversation between Mrs. Li and one of her customers. I kept walking, waiting for Neenie a little further down the block. Being invisible, she could get away standing beside them while they talked, but I sure couldn't.

When she joined me, tucking her hand in my arm, she lifted her face for a kiss. I was happy to oblige, but then I realized that something had changed about her. It had happened so gradually that I'd never noticed. Those blue-blue eyes of hers were almost violet now and I remembered what Ernie had told me, all those months ago.

Something tightened uncomfortably, deep in my chest.

"You…are you going away?" I asked.

"I have to go away," she said. "That's what we do. We're here and then we go away. You do, too."

"But…"

"I know. You're here walking around ever so much longer than we are. But it's still the same."

"You…die?

She frowned, still looking so pretty. "If you mean, do we move from one world to another, then yes. We do. But we don't think of it like that at all. It's just a part of the whole long story of our lives."

"How…how long do we have?"

"We're leaving when the days start to get longer again."

She meant the winter solstice. It was less than two weeks away.

I thought knowing this would change everything, and I did brood about it when we weren't together, but it's impossible to have a heavy heart when you're actually around the gemmin. Ernie was right about that, too.

On the night of the winter solstice, there came a tapping on my window and I looked up to see Neenie's face at my window. I don't know how she got up to a third floor window, but I hurried over to open it and let her in. A gust of cold wind rushed inside and made me shiver. Neenie leaned in, resting her elbows on the sill.

"We're going," she said. "Come meet me on the roof."

Then she did this sort of Spider-Man swing and went monkeying up the side of my building. I didn't hesitate. I put on a coat and shoes and snuck out of the apartment, heading for the stairs.

I thought we'd said goodbye this afternoon when I saw the group of them in the alley by their car. The parting hadn't been hard—my sadness pushed away by their presence—but I'd spent the evening feeling bleaker and bleaker before she showed up at my window.

She was waiting for me on the roof, standing out of the wind beside the little structure that's up there enclosing the top of the stairs. I shivered in the wind as I stepped out the door and joined her, knowing she'd picked this spot for my sake, not hers. She was still just wearing her baggy pants and that little shirt that showed her stomach. The only tracks in the snow leading to where we stood were mine.

"There's something wrong inside me," she said. "I don't know what it is. It feels big and heavy and sometimes it makes it hard to breathe." She lifted her hand to her eyes. "And tears keep wanting to leak out of my eyes."

I knew exactly what she meant. I'd been feeling that way all night.

"Is this what sadness feels like?" she asked.

"That's what it feels like for me."

"It's funny. I've heard about it in a lot of the stories I've collected, but I never knew what it felt like before." She sighed. "It's so heavy."

"I know."

I put my arms around her and held her close. I'd been trying to not cry all night myself.

"It's weighing me down," she said into my shoulder, her sweet, spicy breath lifting to my nose. "It's so heavy that I don't think I can go."

I felt my heart lift. But then she added:

"The others will have to go on without me."

"But…"

I couldn't imagine her on her own. The gemmin were such a close-knit group. Neenie and I had spent a lot of time together, but most of the time we were with the others. I think they needed to be together because I'd noticed that when Neenie and I spent too long a time away from the others, Neenie would start to get quieter and quieter. No less sweet, no less loving. But a stillness would gather around her that became poignant and unfamiliar.

"Troon said you could help me," she said. She lifted her face to look into my eyes. "Is it true? Can you help me feel not so heavy?"

I didn't want to, but I knew what I had to do. I had to let her go.

"I love you, Neenie," I told her. "And I'll always remember you. But you have to go."

"Do you want me to go?"

I shook my head. "But you have to. It's..." I had to swallow. "What you do."

"It is, isn't it?" she said in a small voice.

When she looked up, those violet eyes of hers were shiny with tears, reflecting the streetlights from below. I nodded.

"And you really love me, like people do?"

"I do."

"And you'll really remember me forever and ever and always?"

"I really will."

She gave me a small smile. "I still feel sad."

"Yeah, me, too. But...I feel glad, too. I would never want to have missed out meeting you and knowing you and loving you. You're the best thing that ever happened to me."

"But now I'm going. Doesn't that take away from the happiness?"

I shook my head. "Nothing can take that away."

We held each other for a long moment, the wind rushing across the roof, but not touching us. Then I felt a presence. I turned and the others were there. Troon and Alaween. Mita and Omal and Shivy.

Troon walked up to me and kissed me on the brow.

"Thank you," Troon said. "We would have missed her so terribly. And she...she would have..."

"I know," I said.

One by one the others came up and gave me a kiss and a hug. And then there was just my Neenie.

"You think of me, too," I told her.

"Oh, I couldn't not," she said. "You're the biggest part of all the stories I carry inside me."

Then she kissed me, too, long and hard and sweet.

And they were gone.

I stood there, staring across the city, alone except for the wind, then I went back downstairs to my bedroom.

Ernie was wrong, I thought, as I sat at my desk. They don't break your heart. They fill it up and the memory of that never goes away. Not unless you let it.

I took out a pad and a pen and I started to write.

I went to Ernie's apartment on boxing day. I brought him a wrapped-up box with some of my Mom's baklava in it and his face lit up with pleasure when he took off the wrapping and opened the box.

"I can't remember the last time somebody gave me a Christmas present," he said.

He took me into his kitchen and made us some tea. We talked awhile, about the neighbourhood. Like him, I'd learned to pay attention to all the small stories that ebbed and flowed through its blocks—something we'd learned from the gemmin. It was just a natural part of our lives now.

"They're gone again," he said after awhile.

I nodded. "They left on the solstice."

"Any regrets?"

"Not one. No, maybe one. That I couldn't go with them."

"Yeah, I know that feeling." He hesitated for a moment, then leaned forward across the kitchen table. "Don't end up like me, Ahmad. Don't let this define your life. The neighbourhood doesn't need another guy like me."

"Not even when you're gone?"

"Hey, I'm not that old."

"I know." I looked down at my tea, then back at him. "Just before Christmas break my English teacher gave me this flyer…about a workshop that's going to be at the library in the new year."

"What kind of workshop?"

"For people who want to be writers. It's being given by this local writer named Christy Riddell, so I took out a couple of his books from the library, and you know what? He's got a story in one of them about the gemmin. He didn't see them, but a friend of his did and he wrote about it."

"So you're going to be a writer?"

"I don't know. I'm going to try. My parents'll hate the idea. They're pretty set on me being a doctor or a lawyer. Somebody important."

"Maybe they'll surprise you."

"Maybe."

"Are you going to write about the gemmin?"

"I'm going to write about all the things that people don't pay attention to."

Ernie smiled. "So am I going to be in the story?"

"Yeah, but don't worry. I'll change your name."

"Don't," he said. "I'd be proud to be in your story. Only..."

"Only what?" I asked when his voice trailed off.

"Could you mention Mixie?"

"Was she the one you fell in love with?'

He nodded. "They're all dear to me—from the first ones I met to every new bunch that comes along. But I think you only ever get that one special connection."

"I'll mention her," I told him.

And I did.

# Da Slockit Light

*Da Slockit Light* ("The Putting Out
of the Light") is a Shetland fiddle tune
composed by Tom Anderson.

"**H**ey!" the boy cried.

She wasn't quick enough to stop his hand from darting in and out of her purse, but she managed to snag him by the collar of his shirt before he could get away. She almost hauled him off his feet as she pulled him back towards her. Her wallet fell from his hand. The soft slap as it hit the pavement was lost in the sound of the traffic going by on Lakeside Drive.

"Well, now," Meran Kelledy said, studying her captive.

The boy struggled ineffectively. For all her slenderness, her fingers had an iron grip.

"What have we got here?"

Not much, if looks were anything to go by. He was a homely, under-sized boy in oversized skater's jeans and a plain white T-shirt that was also too big. One running shoe had a grubby toenail poking through its toe, its mate was held together with twine. His hair was an unkempt, brown thatch; his eyes too old.

He couldn't have been much more than twelve or thirteen. If that.

"Lemme go," he demanded.

Retaining her hold on the collar of his shirt, Meran stooped to retrieve her wallet. She flipped it open as she straightened, letting its contents flutter to the pavement.

"Here's what you were stealing," she said.

The boy gave her a look that plainly put her on a level of intelligence just a step up from a slug as he stared at what had fallen from her wallet.

Pressed leaves and bits of paper with what looked like verses scribbled on them; a carefully folded candywrapper; a red balloon and a yellowed newspaper clipping. The only currency was a pair of copper pennies that winked up at them from amongst the detritus.

"That's just crap," he said.

Meran smiled. "Then why did you want to steal it?"

"I...."

Confusion washed across his face, then he spat at her. As she dodged the phlegm, he kicked out at her. The toe of the twine-wrapped runner connected with her shin. Her grip loosened momentarily on his collar and he was off, scurrying down the street, shouting a string of obscenities behind him.

Meran was half-inclined to chase after him, but settled on simply watching until he rounded a corner and was lost from her view.

He was so young....

She stooped once more, this time to retrieve the contents of her wallet, carefully replacing each item.

"Louie Felden," a voice said.

Meran looked up to find a young woman standing close by. She had a face shaped like a heart, short blond hair and pale blue eyes. Her trim figure was lost in a pair of baggy black jean overalls under which she wore a man's dress shirt. A red canvas knapsack hung from her shoulder by one strap, the thumb of her right hand hooked into the bottom of the strap's loop.

"I beg your pardon?" Meran said.

The woman nodded down the street with her chin.

"The boy," she said. "His name's Louie Felden. He does that a lot. Usually he gets away with it."

Meran straightened up. "But he's only a child."

"He's actually around sixteen," the woman said. "But he does look a lot younger." She held out her hand. "My name's Lisa—Lisa Hooper. I used to be his family's social worker. But when his mother died and his father went to prison, he and his brother took to the streets and we couldn't help them. Every time we found a home for them, they'd run away. He'll still talk to me from time to time, when he wants to cadge a meal. But since his brother Bobby died, this is the closest I usually get to him—seeing the back of his head as he runs away."

"I see," Meran said, though she didn't at all.

"Did he get away with anything?"

Meran stowed her wallet back into her purse and shook her head.

"Odd kinds of things to be carrying around in a wallet," Lisa said.

She spoke as though she was trying to keep the conversation going, but wasn't quite ready to get to the point.

"Memories," Meran said.

"Treasure."

They both smiled and Meran decided she liked this woman.

"I saw your concert at the Standish on the weekend," Lisa went on. "You and your husband. I love that kind of music."

"We've been playing it for a very long time."

"And you do it very well."

"Thank you."

"I...."

As Lisa hesitated, Meran knew that she was finally coming to the point of her conversation. She gave Lisa an encouraging smile.

"Working on the street as I do," Lisa went on finally, "I've heard about you and your husband. How you sometimes help people...."

Meran raised an eyebrow.

"I could really use some help," Lisa said.

Meran tucked her hand into the crook of the woman's arm.

"Well, why don't we find someplace quiet," she said, "and you can tell me about it."

It was a short walk up Battersfield Road to Kathryn's Café in the heart of Lower Crowsea. Like the area itself, with its narrow streets and old stone buildings, Kathryn's had an old-world feel about it—from the dark wood paneling and hand-carved chair backs to the small round tables with their checkered tablecloths, fat glass condiment containers and the straw-wrapped wine bottles used as candleholders. The music piped in over the house sound system was timeless. Teleman and Vivaldi, Bill Evans and Clifford Brown.

But if the atmosphere was Old World, the clientele were definitely contemporary. Situated so close to Butler University, Kathryn's had been a favorite haunt of the university students since it first opened in the early sixties as a coffeehouse. Though much had changed from those early days, there was still live music played on its small stage on Friday and Saturday nights, as well as poetry recitations on Wednesdays and Sunday morning storytelling sessions.

Meran and Lisa sat by a window, fair trade coffee and homemade banana muffins set out on the table in front of them.

"How much do you know of Newford history?" Lisa asked after she'd stirred her coffee for the third time.

"Well, I don't follow politics."

"But you've heard of Old City?"

Meran nodded. Old City was part of the original heart of Newford. It lay underneath the subway tunnels—dropped there in the late eighteen hundreds during the great quake. The present city, including its sewers and underground transportation tunnels, had been built above the ruins of the old. There'd been talk in the early seventies of renovating the ruins as a tourist attraction—as had been done in Seattle—but Old City lay too far underground for easy access, and after numerous studies on the project, the city council had decided that it simply wouldn't be cost-effective.

"There've always been stories about people living down there," Lisa went on. "You know, skells—winos and bag ladies and the like. But now I keep hearing rumours on the streets that if you're lost and hurt and nobody cares about you—you can find a haven in Old City." Lisa gave Meran a wan smile. "You know—like on that old TV show with the cat guy."

Meran shook her head. "We've never had a television."

"Oh." Lisa blinked, as though the concept of not owning a set was utterly foreign to her. "Well, it's supposed to be a kind of utopia. Dry and warm. You don't have to worry about food, or police, or parents...."

Her voice trailed off.

"And?" Meran prompted her after a few moments of silence.

"I don't believe in benevolent utopias," Lisa said, "but I do believe that something's going on down there and it can't be good. Street people are disappearing. *Kids* are disappearing. It's not in the papers, because the press hasn't caught on to it yet, but I hear the talk around the office. I'm not the only one whose caseload has suddenly lightened. Everybody I work with has heard these new stories about Old City."

"So why don't you go to the papers?"

Lisa shook her head. "And tell them what? Even a rag like *The Examiner* is going to want more than the say-so of a few social workers."

"Well, then, how about the police?"

"We're talking street people and poverty level families that are probably relieved to have a mouth less to feed."

"I can't believe that," Meran said.

Though what she really meant was, she didn't want to believe it.

"I've seen parents sell their own kids," Lisa said. A bleakness settled in her eyes. "I'm not saying they're all like that, but there are people out there with children who shouldn't be entrusted with the responsibility of caring for a goldfish, little say a child. In a city this big you're going to get all kinds—and that includes the dregs."

"Still, the police—"

"Missing person reports have been filed, but they're all caught up in paperwork."

Meran sighed and looked out the window. Across the street, two children were playing ball in an alleyway.

"What did you want me to do?" she asked finally.

Lisa shook her head. "I don't know. I just heard you could fix things. I thought maybe you could look into it. I just want to know that they're…okay."

"What makes you think they're not?"

"They don't come back."

"I see," Meran said. "I'll talk to my husband. And we'll see what we can do."

"Here's my card," Lisa said. "Call me if you need anything."

Meran turned the card over and over in her hands, her gaze drifting across the street again to where the children played. A prickle of uneasiness fingered her spine.

"We'll do what we can," she said softly.

When she got home, Meran followed the sound of harping through the house until she came to the narrow, windowless room on the second floor that her husband used for his music. It was just large enough for a few comforts and necessities: a Morris chair with a reading lamp standing behind it; a barrister's bookcase that stood five stacks high, the middle shelf of which had a wooden front that folded out to make a small desk; and his roseharp, Teleynros, standing near the straight-backed chair he sat in when he played. The bookcases were stuffed with music folios, mostly written in his hand. More lay in stacks on the floor, or balanced precariously from the ledge of his music stand.

There were many rooms in this big rambling house of theirs, rooms with tall ceilings and wonderful acoustics, with windows that overlooked the gardens along the sides and back, or the grove of oak trees in front. But for some reason, this was the room Cerin preferred.

He looked up when she reached the doorway.

"That's the tune you taught Alan, isn't it?"

Cerin nodded. "'Eliz Iza.' He plays it so simply, yet I can't seem to capture the poetry he puts into it."

"Different hearts make different music."

He smiled.

"I was talking to a social worker today," Meran said.

"One of Angel's people?"

"No. Her name's Lisa and she works for the city. She was telling me about this community of homeless people and runaways that's living in Old City."

"There've always been stories of people living down there and in the abandoned subway tunnels."

Meran nodded. "But for that many people to be down there, they'll have started to encroach—"

"On goblin territory. What does Christy call them?"

"Skookin," Meran said with a smile.

"That's it. And our friend Bramley's butler is their king, isn't he? I'm surprised he'd let any more than a few stragglers take refuge down there."

Notoriously bad-tempered, Olaf Goonasekara was not known for either his generosity or patience.

"The problem," Meran went on, "is that the people going down there don't seem to be coming back."

"Maybe I'll take a walk down there. I'll see if Lucius feels like going for a stroll."

While her husband didn't have Goon's unfortunate temperament, he could be infuriatingly protective. He grinned now at the look on her face.

"It's for simple reconnaissance," he said. "There'd be nothing strange about a couple of odd birds like Lucius and myself wandering about down there. We do that kind of thing all the time. But a lady such as yourself, who loves the woods and the open air? What would they make of your wandering about in that dark Goblinburg? If there is anything suspicious, your appearance would immediately raise an alarm."

"I suppose…"

"And considering your history…" he added.

"Yes, well…"

"Not to mention that Old Town's under the ground."

Meran nodded. She rode the subway as rarely as possible, preferring streetcars and buses, and she hated basements. It was the being underground. In her father's forest, their trees sent roots deep into the earth, wandering happily down there in the dirt and rocks, but the people lived above ground. She felt more kinship to the boughs that reached skyward, and the leaves that exchanged their gossips with the wind.

"But it's not like I *can't* go underground," she said.

"I know. Only why go, if you don't need to?"

So she agreed to stay home, and the two of them went down into Old City, her tall harper husband and Lucius Portsmouth, a large black Buddha of a man with pure raven blood and such a brood of relatives, it was impossible to keep track of them all.

And they didn't come back.

Meran was looking through the vegetable drawer in the fridge to see if she had enough for a stir fry, when her flute came scampering in. It wasn't in flute form when it was mobile like this, of course, but rather in its bodach shape: Wee Jack, skinny as a stick figure with a narrow head and large eyes.

"Mistress, mistress!" the little man called. "The goblins have himself."

The big rambling Kelledy house was home to dozens of bodachs and other fairy folk. They loved to tease Meran, but kept out of her husband's way, since they believed his harping could lock them into an inanimate form. A superstitious bunch, they wouldn't even use his name in conversation, referring to Cerin as "himself" instead.

Meran looked up from her inventory.

"What did you say?"

"I'm sorry, I'm sorry," Wee Jack said, "but I heard it from Caperdrum, who heard it from the Church Street wrens, who heard a pair of goblins talking about it not a half hour ago."

Meran banged the fridge door shut and ran up the stairs to Cerin's music room to check on the roseharp. She already feared the worst because, now that she was listening for it, she realized that the instrument's usual murmuring had gone still. That never happened. No matter where Cerin was, there was a bond between himself and his harp that kept the strings of the instrument trembling, if not actually playing some soft tune—no matter where or how far away Cerin might have gone.

But it was silent now.

She walked slowly up to the harp and put a hand on its support beam, close to where the rose was carved out of the joint. Against her palm, the wood felt cool, rather than the warmth of an instrument in use.

Wee Jack stood miserable in the doorway, unwilling, as most of the house's uninvited inhabitants would be, to actually enter the master's private room.

"Oh, what will we do?" he asked.

Meran regarded him with dark eyes.

"Pay a visit to Old City," she said.

Wee Jack gave her a look as though he thought she'd gone mad.

"But if they've captured himself and Mr. Raven..."

Meran gave a slow nod. Old as time, the pair had more magic in a little finger than an oak maid might in her whole tree, just saying she even had a tree anymore. If the goblins had found a way to render them captive, they'd make even quicker work of her.

"Then maybe we should pay a visit to their king," she said.

Wee Jack shivered, but this time he made no argument.

"Is Goon here?" Meran demanded when the door to the professor's house opened at her knock.

Jilly Coppercorn stood in the doorway, leaning on a pair of canes, and smiled at her.

"And hello to you, too," she said.

It took Meran a moment to shift from fierce mode.

"I'm sorry," she said. "It's just that his goblins have done something to Cerin and Lucius."

Jilly's eyes widened with concern. Using her canes, she shuffled to one side as quickly as she could make herself move.

"He's in the kitchen," she said.

Meran thanked her, then swept down the hall, with a little fairy man at her heels. The little man waved to Jilly as he hurried along behind his mistress, leaving Jilly blinking and not entirely sure she'd even seen him. By the time she got to the kitchen, Meran had the professor's butler backed up against one of the kitchen's counters.

"Did you forget who we were?" Meran was saying in a grim voice that Jilly had never heard her use before. "Do you think I wouldn't be able to remember the word that will unmake you?"

Jilly had grown so used to thinking of the professor's friends as people she just sat around with, sharing a cup of tea and some gossip, she'd forgotten that so many of them had truly exotic origins. Meran was a dryad from the Otherworld, her husband an ageless harper. Goon—properly Olaf Goonasekara, though no one called him that—was the king of the skookin who lived under the streets of Newford in Old City. Lucius was the Raven who'd called the world into being, though he himself didn't remember that. He had that in common with the crow girls, who were almost never aware of being anything other than a pair of rambunctious teenage girls.

But Jilly hadn't realized that Meran Kelledy had a temper or could be so grim, because in all the time Jilly had known her, Meran had only ever been kind and sweet-mannered. Such wasn't the case now. Today she was in full mother bear mode, protecting those she loved.

"I have nothing to do with the world down under," Goon protested.

In place of his usual curmudgeonly demeanor, he actually looked alarmed. Jilly didn't blame him. She was feeling a bit worried herself, and Meran's attention wasn't even on her.

"It's common knowledge that you rule in Goblinburg," Meran said.

"Then it should be equally common knowledge that my throne was taken from me and Cornig Fairnswanter sits on it in my place."

"You abdicated?"

Goon shrugged. He was regaining some of the normal sour look that he normally wore.

"As much as, I suppose," he said. "By choosing to live here with Bramley, rather than down under."

Meran's shoulders lost their stiff resolve and drooped.

"And this Fairnswanter," she said. "How did he become so powerful that he could trap both Cerin and Lucius?"

Goon shook his head. "The Fairnswanter I knew couldn't have. He's nothing more than a little pissant with a couple of drops of royal Goonasekara blood from a few generations back."

"They're changing human folk into goblins down there," a small voice piped up.

Jilly tracked it to its source and saw the little man who'd come in with Meran standing on one of the kitchen chairs. Meran's gaze followed Jilly's.

"Where did you hear that?" Meran asked.

The little man shrugged. "It's just something everybody knows."

"And you never told me?"

"I thought you knew, Mistress. I thought everybody knew."

"I didn't," Goon said.

"Oh, it's all darkness and trouble down below," the little man said. "No one goes there now—not among my folk."

"None of this was my doing," Goon said.

Meran nodded. "I can see that now."

"I don't particularly like humans, but—"

"Then again, you don't like anyone," Meran finished for him.

Goon gave her a haughty look.

"I was going to say, I don't agree with reshaping of any kind—simply on principal. Alchemy's best left in the box with all the other perils men have inflicted on the world."

"What makes you think this is alchemy?" Meran asked.

"Human into skookin's no different than iron into gold. What would you call it?"

Jilly made her way to the table and carefully lowered herself into one of the free chairs. She leaned her canes up against the table and rubbed her right arm. It was tingling from the strain of using the cane, all the way from her shoulder to the tips of her fingers.

"I don't suppose anyone wants to tell me what's going on?" she asked.

Three heads turned in her direction. For a moment, Jilly thought no one was going to answer, but then Meran pulled out a chair. Sitting down, she told what had happened, frowning at Goon when she got to the part about what Wee Jack had heard.

"I've been down below twice before," she said, finishing up. "Once with you, Jilly, to bring back that drum you'd inadvertently borrowed, and once to get back a hair comb that had been borrowed from me." That earned Goon another dark look. "But on neither trip did I see or hear of anything with enough power down there to capture both my husband and Lucius."

"Neither have I," Goon said, "and I know the secrets of Old City. Something new has taken up residence there."

"And been welcomed by your people," Meran said.

"Or has bent them to its will." Goon turned to Wee Jack. "And you say they're swelling goblin ranks with human changelings?"

The little man nodded.

"I don't understand," Meran said. "What would be the point? Surely they don't think they could raise an army against the human world?"

"I doubt it," Goon said. "But there hasn't been a child born down below in over fifty years old. There was always talk—even when I lived down below—of how to find new blood to replace those who have died."

"Well, it appears that now they have."

"Indeed."

Meran straightened in her chair. "And I suppose now I'll have to go and find out what."

"You can't," Goon said. "If they took the other two so easily—"

"We don't know how easily they were taken."

"—then they will take you, too. And your old words of power will be of no use to you down below. Speak one of them there and you'll bring the new city down upon the old, and upon your own head as well."

"Can you go?" Meran asked.

Goon shook his head. "I'm too well known, and probably less welcome. What we need is a thief. Someone to creep in and snoop about for us. Until we know *what* we're dealing with, we can't make any plans."

He and Meran both turned to Wee Jack.

"Why are you looking at me?" he asked.

"Because," Goon said, "sneaky thief is the very definition of a bodach."

"Oh, unlike a skookin, who's the soul of good manners and means no one any harm."

"I thought skookin was a word Christy or the professor made up," Jilly said, hoping to forestall an argument between the two.

"Where is Bramley?" Meran asked before either Goon or Wee Jack could speak.

"Delivering a paper on his Bigfoot theories at some conference in Anchorage," Jilly told her.

Goon snorted. "It's not a conference. It's one of those sci-fi conventions where people dress up like spacemen or—"

"Ill-mannered skookin," Wee Jack offered.

"Better that, than a cowardly bodach."

"I'm not cowardly," Wee Jack said. He turned to Meran. "Am I, Mistress?"

"Not in the least."

"It's just, if there's dark magic afoot, they'll sniff me out, in the down below. We always know when there's other fairy about, so the skookin will, too."

"That's true," Goon had to admit.

"I know a thief," Meran said. "A human one. Just tell me what he needs to look for, where he needs to go."

If Louie Felden felt any surprise at Meran tracking him down in his Tombs squat, it didn't show in his features. He didn't get up when she stepped over the litter in the doorway and entered his room. The only furnishings were a pile of trash in one corner, the duffel bag he was using as a pillow, and the bedding on which he sat.

"Did you bring the police?" he asked.

"No. Should I have?"

He shrugged. "I'm not going anywhere with you, if that's what you're thinking. I'm not going to be anybody's project. I'm not something you can fix."

"Actually, I'm here to avail myself of your expertise."

"Say what?"

"I want to know if you'll do a job for me."

He gave her a considering look and followed it with another shrug.

"What do you want me to steal?" he asked.

"Nothing. It's more like a scouting expedition."

He sat up straighter, interested despite himself. "To where?"

"Old City."

"Ah. You've been talking to Lisa."

"I have," Meran agreed. "But not about this."

He lounged back against his duffel bag.

"Maybe," he said, "people just like it better down there and that's why they're not coming back."

Meran nodded. "And maybe something's keeping them down there against their will. Maybe they're being...changed."

"Maybe, but why should you care? There's all kinds of homeless people who aren't going down into Old City who'd be happy to become your personal charity cases. Want me to point out a few of them to you?"

"My husband's down there," Meran told him.

Louie shook his head. "You don't look the type to have a wino for an old man, but then I guess it doesn't matter how high and mighty a person might be before they find themselves on the streets—you hit the bottom just the same."

"It's not like that."

"Look at me," he said. "This is where I live. You've already seen how I make my living. You don't have to be embarrassed in front of someone like me. Shit happens. Whatever he's done with his life, it's not necessarily your fault."

"I know. But it really isn't like that. Someone is keeping him down there."

"And you want me to bring him back?"

"I doubt that would be possible, and I wouldn't ask you to get so involved. I just want you to go down there and snoop around, see if you can find out what's happening."

"And then?" he asked.

"You come back and tell me."

He studied her for a long moment, then shook his head.

"Nah, I don't think so," he told her. "You seem like a nice lady, but I try not to get involved in other people's problems. There's nothing in it for me."

"I'll give you a hundred dollars to go down. More when you get back and bring me something useful."

"A hundred dollars?"

She nodded.

"Right now—*before* I go?"

When she nodded again, he just laughed.

"What's to stop me from just taking your money and blowing you off?" he asked.

"I'd find you and get it back."

"Yeah, right."

"I found you here, didn't I?"

He frowned. "How did you track me down?"

Meran nodded to the window.

"The gargoyle across the street told me you were here," she said.

He laughed again. "Oh, right. The gargoyle."

But he got up and had a look out the window. The abandoned structure across the street from his squat had once been an office building and there was a gargoyle pushing out from its roof gutter that had a direct view into his window. There were, in fact, three of them along the gutter, each a little more grotesque than the next.

He was still smiling when he turned back to Meran. She returned his smile and pulled a hundred dollar bill from her pocket and offered it to him.

"You're awfully trusting," he said. "I could just roll you for whatever else you're carrying."

"Try me," she said.

He tried to stare her down, but he couldn't hold her gaze as long as she could his.

"Whatever," he said.

Walking over from the window, he plucked the bill from her hand.

"So how do I get in touch with you?" he asked.

"Call my name aloud three times. Someone will hear and tell me."

"Ho-kay."

"Thank you, Louie," she said, then picked her way back over the litter in his doorway and returned the way she'd come.

Louie stood in his squat, turning the hundred dollar bill over in his hands. Then something occurred to him. He went to the door to call down the hall that she hadn't told him her name.

But she was already gone.

An hour later, Louie was in Jimmy's Billiards at the corner of Vine and Palm, halfway to doubling his money in a game with three college kids too green to realize they were being sharked by what they thought was some dumb little kid. Jimmy'd been letting him hang around the pool hall for years, even though he was underage. They had an understanding.

Louie could play the tables, but if he so much as tried to have a sip from anybody's drink, he was out on his ass.

Seemed fair to Louie. He didn't like the taste of beer anyway. What he liked was this: playing the game, sinking the impossible shots.

He was about to take a complicated cross-side when a strong hand clapped onto his shoulder.

"The fuck?" he said.

He slipped out of the grip and turned, trying to get the room to bring his pool cue into play and give whoever this was a lesson in manners, except it was only her. That weird woman who'd tracked him down in his squat.

"I meant do it immediately," she said.

"Okay, this is getting creepy," he told her. "How'd you—"

She stepped in close to him. "Or you can just give me my money back."

"Lady, you need to back off," he said and started to give her a push.

He didn't get to touch her. She caught his wrist before his hand could reach her shoulder, and just like that, he couldn't move his arm.

"I'm disappointed," she said. "I thought you were a man of your word."

He pulled back, but he couldn't get his wrist free until she decided to let it go. The college kids were watching all of this with big eyes. Hell, everybody in Jimmy's was watching him be humiliated. But that didn't make him feel as bad as what she'd said. He wanted to tell her that you only kept your word to your brothers and sisters on the street, not some chump woman like her. Except he knew that wasn't true. Your word was your word. And she wasn't a chump. He didn't know what the hell she was, but she wasn't some mark, ready to be fleeced.

"I...I didn't know you were in such a big hurry," he said.

"I am."

He tried to hold her gaze and again he was the first to look away.

"Whatever," he said.

He peeled off a few bills from his winnings and tossed them on the green velvet to cover the table.

"Some other time, guys," he said. "Duty calls."

One of the college boys—the one who'd come in with the lettered jacket—laughed.

"Yeah," he said. "You wouldn't want to keep Mommy waiting for that little dick of yours."

His friends began to laugh with them until Meran turned in their direction and fixed them with her dark gaze.

Crap, Louie thought. Now it was going to get messy, because he was going to have to hit that loudmouth, just on general principle.

Except before he could step in, Jimmy himself was standing at the side of the table, a half-smoked cigar stuck out of the corner of his mouth.

"These guys bothering you, Meran?" he asked the woman.

"Oh, I don't think they're going to be any trouble—are you boys?"

Here and there in the pool room, dark-skinned men were stepping back from their tables, or standing up from the benches where they'd been drinking beer and watching the various games.

The college boys were green, but they weren't entirely stupid.

"Sorry, ma'am," the one who'd spoken up first said. "I didn't mean anything by that."

"You see, Jimmy?" the woman said. "'Everything's fine.'"

The college boys beat a hasty retreat. Jimmy returned to his stool behind the bar. The men who'd displayed such a sudden interest were back doing what they'd been doing as though they'd never interrupted their activities.

Louie suppressed a shiver. There was something seriously *weird* going on here.

When the woman started for the door, Louie followed her.

"So how do you know Jimmy?" he asked as they walked down the stairs to the street.

"Oh, Jimmy knows everybody," she said over her shoulder.

"Yeah, I guess he does." Though how would he know someone like you, Louie wanted to ask. Instead he said, "And all those guys who seemed so interested?"

She stopped on the sidewalk and gave him a guileless look.

"Oh, you know how it is," she said. "Sometimes people just get protective."

Yeah, but not toughs like that. He'd seen some of those same guys just sit there and watch somebody get beat half to death without lifting a hand to stop it.

"So," the woman went on. "Do we still have a bargain?"

"Yeah, sure."

"Then, please," she said. "Would you get to it?"

And then she walked off down the street.

Louie stood there for a long moment, watching her go.

You owe me some explanations, lady, he thought.

But he turned and headed for the Grasso Street subway station. There was a steel door in its east tunnel that led down into Old City. There were probably other ways down, but that was the only one he knew.

And that was how Louie found himself skulking around through the rubbled streets of Old City, wondering what exactly he was doing down here. It had started with a hundred bucks, but it wasn't about the money anymore. Now it was about keeping his word, and what was up with that?

He'd only been down here a couple of times before, just to check it out, but he'd never stayed. This was where the real losers came, the people with no hope at all. It wasn't particularly great, squatting in the abandoned buildings of the Tombs, but you could still pretend you were semi-normal. You could drift out of the ruined blocks of old tenements, factories and office buildings and take your tithe from the normal citizens who had real homes to go to. A little panhandling, some wallet snatching, pool sharking if you had enough cash to stake you a game.

Old City was where you went when you just gave up.

The door from the subway station opened into what had once been a four-story building before the quake dropped it underground. Louie made his way down a stairwell that years of previous visitors had cleaned up enough so that the route was relatively clear. When he stepped out of the building, he was on the ruin of an old lost street.

Which was really more weirdness, when you thought about it.

Louie looked around himself.

How come he'd never thought about this the other times he'd been here? He was deep underground, but it wasn't completely dark like it should be. Once your eyes adjusted, you could make out the buildings, the rubble on the street around you. And what was a street doing here? How come the buildings still stood? How come everything wasn't just buried and swallowed away in the dirt?

He craned his neck and stared up into the dark, but he couldn't see a roof. Couldn't see anything up there.

He shrugged. Whatever. And started off down the street.

There weren't a lot of people living down here, but after a couple of blocks, he was surprised that he hadn't run into anybody. The other times, he'd seen people huddled in doorways, ducking out of sight in windows, scurrying down narrow alleys. Today there was nothing.

He'd walked for about ten minutes before he saw the glow of a fire ahead. He quickened his pace until he was close enough to see that the fire was in an old oil drum. Some guy stood by it, warming his hands.

Louie looked around himself, blinking at the afterimages the fire had put in his gaze. The guy seemed to be on his own, so Louie approached him, walking easy, hands in his pockets, one wrapped around the handle of the flick-knife he kept in his right jacket pocket.

What a weird looking little guy, Louie thought. He had a big round head and a bigger rounded body, with not much of a neck in between, so he looked like two-thirds of a snow man. His arms and legs, in sharp contrast, were thin as twigs. But he seemed friendly enough, smiling as Louie approached.

"Got any food?" the guy asked.

Louie pulled a chocolate bar from his left pocket and passed it over.

"Thanks, kid."

"No problem." He looked around himself. "So where is everybody?"

"This is Old City, kid," the guy told him around a mouthful of chocolate. "You don't exactly get crowds around here."

"Yeah, but I haven't seen a soul. Usually there's somebody around."

"I'm here, ain't I? Stadell Froome, at your service."

"You know what I mean," Louie said.

Froome nodded with his head, indicating where the city went on.

"Folks have been taking to heading on," he said, "and they don't come back."

"Something happening to them?"

"I guess you could say that. There's a bunch living down there that can fix people so they're more comfortable living here below. Use a thing they've got called da slockit light to get the job done."

"That supposed to mean something?"

Froome nodded. "It's a thing that puts out the light we carry inside us—you know, like your soul?—but you don't die the way you normally would when you lose that light. You just get changed."

"Changed into what?"

"Like I said: into something that's more comfortable living down here."

Louie shook his head. "Why would anybody want to do a thing like that?"

"You've got a lot of questions, kid."

Louie shrugged. "I'm just curious. Curiosity's the only thing I haven't lost yet, I guess."

"People come down here, they don't have *anything* left."

"Yeah, well I'm not planning to move in. I'm just snooping around. I've got no home, no job, and no money, so bumming around and snooping into weird-ass shit's pretty much all that's left to fill my day."

Froome laughed. "Guess you've got a point, kid."

"So how do the people find out about this thing that can change them? They just go wandering around until they stumble onto it?"

"Nah. There's these guys come up through here from time to time. They talk it up, offer to show anybody who's interested how they can partake of it their own selves."

Louie smiled. "These guys look anything like you?"

"Now that you mention it, maybe they do. I could show you, if you're interested. I owe you a favour, after all, for that very tasty chocolate bar that was freely given."

There was something about the way he said "freely given" that set off a little warning bell in Louie's head. It was the same one that went off when he was setting up a pool game and he realized the other player was playing him.

"I don't think showing me anything's worth the favour you owe me," he said. "Not when it's something you'd do anyway."

Something flickered in Froome's eyes, but it was gone before Louie could read it.

"Got me there, kid," he said. "You want to see it anyway?"

"What? This socket light?"

Froome shook his head. "That's 'slockit light' and it's all got to do with the light you've got inside you. The thing we've got back there can put it out for you. Stop the hurting, you know? Up above—" he nodded with his head "—no one gives a crap about what happens to you. They don't get the pain that won't go away, because they're snug in their perfect little lives."

"Everybody feels pain," Louie said.

"Sure, but not everybody's got the nice meal, or the pretty toys, or the soft bed, or the family and friends to help make it go away."

Louie nodded. "You've got a point."

"Course I do, kid. You wouldn't be here if I didn't."

"So what's in it for you?"

Froome looked genuinely puzzled. "What do you mean?"

"Well, you're helping all these people into these new lives of theirs where they can forget about the dark hole in their heads and just be happy down here, right?"

"Right,"

"So what do you get out of it?"

"Company," Froome said.

"Just that."

Froome nodded. "What else? It's not like these people have anything else to offer."

The funny thing was, Louie believed him. Everybody had an angle, he knew that—some way they came out ahead—but Froome seemed to be the exception.

"Cool," he said.

Froome smiled. "So do you want come see how it's done?"

This was the point where he should go back to the woman—what had Jimmy called her? Something like...Marion.

What he should be doing is go back above ground and tell Marion what he'd learned. Show her that he could keep his word, earn his hundred dollars.

But he found himself wanting to do more.

Marion was a woman who obviously knew a lot of other people who could have done this for her. She knew Jimmy. She knew the toughs that hung around the pool hall. But she'd come to him. He'd tried to lift her wallet, but she'd still come to him and offered him good money to do a job for her.

She didn't look at him like he was some little useless kid. She'd looked at him like he was a person. Like he could do this for her. Like he could give his word and keep it.

That hadn't happened in a long, long time.

Most people just wanted to fix him up, like he was broken. He knew he was small for his age—he looked about twelve, but he was actually sixteen now. And he was a homely kid, that was about the kindest way you could put it. "Ugly as sin," was how his old man used to describe him. Sure, he lived on the streets, but he made do. He didn't peddle his ass like Bobby had before he'd ODed. And it wasn't like he really hurt anybody. People could afford what he took. And even when he lifted a wallet, he didn't try to peddle the ID or the credit cards. He just took the cash and dropped the wallet in the nearest mailbox.

So he wasn't an angel. But that didn't mean he had nothing to give.

He could do this thing: find out what was going on, maybe track down Marion's husband for her, too.

Not to be the hero.

Just to show that he was worth his word, and maybe more. Because he couldn't remember anybody ever having any kind of faith in him before.

"Well?" Froome asked.

Louie shrugged. "Sure, why not? I've come this far, so I might as well check this thing out."

Meran decided she needed to go home, and Jilly thought she shouldn't be on her own. In the end, they all made the trek from the professor's house with Goon pushing Jilly's wheelchair and Wee Jack riding on her lap.

"How come nobody else seems to see him?" Jilly asked when they were on Stanton Street and had passed yet another person oblivious to the little bodach.

"They do," Meran told her. "They just see him in his other form."

Jilly looked down and for a moment she thought there was a wooden flute lying on her lap instead of a little man riding there. Then it was Wee Jack again, grinning up at her.

"He's..."

"My flute, yes," Meran said.

Jilly grinned. "I just love magic."

"We don't," a voice said from above.

Jilly looked up to see the crow girls—two skinny, dark-haired girls perched in the branches of one of Stanton's tall old oak trees. They dropped lightly to the ground and gave Goon fierce looks.

"Magic's just trouble," Maida said.

Zia nodded. "Like goblins stealing away your uncle."

"We're going down there right now."

"We'll set things right."

"We'll bang them with sticks."

Zia waved the twig she had in her hand. "Except I need a bigger stick."

"You can't go down there," Goon said.

Maida stuck out her tongue at him. "We don't have to listen to you."

"No, you're just a goblin yourself."

Zia slapped her twig against the palm of her hand.

"Maybe we'll just bang you with sticks," she added.

"As soon as we get bigger ones," Maida said.

"Much bigger ones."

"Please don't," Meran said.

She explained how, if there was something down below that could render both Cerin and Lucius helpless, then a frontal attack, even by two such brave crow girls, probably wasn't the best idea.

"We're not afraid," Zia said.

"Not one bit."

"Not even a bit of a bit."

"Not even—"

"I know you're not," Meran said. "But I'm asking you to wait. Will you do that for me?"

The crow girls gave Goon another pair of fierce scowls, but they nodded in agreement.

"Maybe you could ask your cousins if there's any news," Meran added.

Looking ahead, Jilly saw that the oaks surrounding the Kelledy house were full of crows. They were making a terrible racket, as though they were all talking at the same time. As she watched, new ones arrived, while others flew off.

"We can do that," Zia said and the two of them ran off ahead.

Meran turned to Goon. "You're lucky they don't remember how powerful they really are."

"I know," Goon said. "I'd be skookin jelly on the sidewalk."

"What do you mean?" Jilly asked.

"The crow girls were already here when Raven made the world," Meran explained. "They're the oldest and most powerful of all, but it's not something they remember."

"Why not?"

"I'm not sure. I think it's got something to with how remembering something like…well, I think it would be too much for anyone to hold onto and still stay sane."

"I'd hardly call that pair sane," Goon muttered.

"I like them," Jilly said.

"You would."

"But why," Jilly asked Meran, "don't you let them go down below? If they're so powerful…"

"There's a story," Meran said, "that if the crow girls ever fully wake and remember who they are, they will return the world to the state it was in before Raven made it."

"That doesn't make any sense. If there was no world until Raven made it…oh, I get it. There'd just be nothing."

Meran nodded.

"Nothing," Goon said, "and the crow girls. *If* those stories are true."

"But they've been fierce before," Jilly said. "I've heard stories of them helping people out of some pretty rough situations."

"That's like you or me, turning in our sleep because of a restless dream. On those occasions you're referring to, I doubt they actually woke up."

Jilly slowly shook her head. "The world really is a complicated place, isn't it?"

"Or a very simple one," Meran said.

She seemed about to say more, but just then the crow girls came racing back, shrieking as raucously as their cousins in the trees above.

"There's news, there's news!" Zia cried.

"But the news is there's no news!" Maida added.

Meran sighed and Jilly's heart went out to her.

Froome led Louie deeper into Old City. After awhile, the rubble-strewn streets gave way to tidier avenues as though city work crews had been down here, cleaning up and maintaining the area. Louie still didn't see anyone about, but now he got the sense that they were no longer alone. That they were being watched from the buildings, even though he could never actually catch a single soul in the act.

Finally they came to a small park. Dead trees were the only vegetation left. In the middle of the park was what looked like a stone table, and on it, a lantern stood amongst a clutter of smaller objects that he couldn't make out from where he was. The lantern itself gave off a strange red light—it made Louie uncomfortable, but it also quickened his pulse.

He wasn't sure he wanted to get any closer to that light, but he followed Froome all the same, his gaze locked onto the lantern's glow until he was distracted by a life-sized stone statue lying on its back not far from the table. He stepped closer and looked down on it. It was a little hard to tell because of the way it was lying there, but it appeared to be a rendering of a man who, if the statue had been set upright, would have been crouching down and looking at something terribly interesting. On his shoulder was a raven. The workmanship was amazing—so much detail. You could make out every feather of the raven's wings, every hair on the man's head.

"Cool statue," Louie said.

He put a hand on the knee closest to him and suddenly heard a voice in his head.

*Who's there?*

It was a day for strangeness, Louie thought, no question about it. Strangest of all, maybe, was how he didn't question the way he was just going along with each new surprise that came his way.

He'd never been particularly imaginative. Oh, he could scheme and plot and work out the finest details of a scam, no problem. But he hadn't had fairy tales read to him as a kid, hadn't really *had* a childhood. So he didn't know how to use his mind for the make-believe that would allow a person to imagine there to be more to the world than what you could see. For Louie, everything just was what it was. He didn't care about its story, just whether it could be of use to him or not. Truth was, he'd never had much of an interest in any kind of story until this strange day came along and woke a hunger in him.

Now he wanted to know the story behind Marion and Jimmy and the dark-skinned men in the pool hall. He wanted to know the story behind Froome and his need to turn the hopeless and the lost into odd little people, just like him. And most of all, at this moment, he wanted to know the story behind the voice in his head which—he had the crazy idea—was coming form the statue his hand was resting upon.

*Can you hear me?* he asked, shaping the words in his head.

*Yes. Who are you?*

*Nobody. But I guess I could be a friend. How can I help you?*
*Break the—*

Louie lost the connection to the voice when Froome grabbed his arm and jerked him back from the statue.

"What are you doing?" Froome wanted to know.

"Nothing," Louie said. "It's just a really interesting statue."

He wanted to put his hand on it again, but Froome was standing between him and the statue now.

"Where did it come from?" he asked Froome.

"Nowhere. It's always been here. It must have been part of the world above and came down when everything else did."

Oh yeah? Louie thought. Then why is it lying on its back when everything else around here has been tidied up and set right?

But all he said was, "I guess. But don't you wonder if—"

He started to reach for the statue again—"Break what?" he wanted to ask the voice—but Froome pushed him away.

"Don't bother with that nosy old thing," Froome said and steered him towards the stone table. "This is what you really came to see."

Louie let himself be led over to the table. This close, the lantern made him more than uncomfortable. The dull red light, like the fading embers in a fire, started a pulsing between his temples. Nausea filled the pit of his stomach like sour milk. He wanted to put his hands on the lantern and let the light run over his skin. At the same time, he wanted to run as far from it as he could. To pay his couple of bucks at the Y and scrub himself in the showers for as long as he could, never mind the creepy guys who hung out in there looking to prey on the little kid he seemed to be.

He forced himself to look away, turning his attention to the junk that was piled around the lantern. The weirdest thing for sure was the mummified hand that gripped the lantern's handle, but the rest of the stuff wasn't exactly treasure. Bottle caps and rats' skulls. Lengths of ribbon, coins and a bird's nest. Feathers, twigs and shoelaces. Screw bits and empty pop cans. Smoothed pebbles, balls of tinfoil, and tangles of rubberbands.

"What is all this crap?" he asked.

Froome shrugged. "People carry around the strangest things—especially those who end up down below. But after the change, they don't seem to need those things anymore."

Like anybody ever would, Louie thought.

Reluctantly, his gaze went back to the lantern. He remembered what the voice in his head had started to say.

*Break the...*

It seemed pretty obvious what it had been trying to tell him to do.

Break the frigging lantern.

Louie didn't have a problem with that. He just had to figure out how to do it before Froome could stop him. He had the feeling the little man was a lot faster and stronger than you'd think.

"Did you hear that?" Meran asked.

The others shook their heads from where they sat around the kitchen table in the Kelledy's house.

"Hear what?" Jilly asked.

Meran was smiling. "The roseharp. It played for a moment."

"Does that mean something?" Goon asked.

"It means the master's still alive!" Wee Jack cried and he jumped down from his chair and did circuit of cartwheels all around the table.

The crow girls got up, too, and danced about, though for their part they weren't so much celebrating as using the news as an excuse to not have to sit still.

"When it was so silent," Meran told Jilly and Goon through the hubbub, "I feared the worst."

Jilly cocked an ear, but she couldn't hear anything above the tumult of the bodach and the crow girls.

"But now you can hear it," she said.

Meran shook her head. "No, but *having* heard it I know that Cerin and Lucius have just been taken away. They're not dead." She looked down the hall. "Oh, I wish Louie would finish so that we can know what we're up against."

"It's been awhile now," Goon said.

"I know," Meran said.

"He could be far away with your money."

Meran nodded. "Except we know that he went down under and the crows haven't seen him come out yet."

"I don't envy him being down there," Jilly said.

"No," Meran said. "Neither do I."

"So how does it work?" Louie asked. "You know, how does it change people?"

Froome didn't answer. He was studying Louie, a strange look in his eyes.

"He doesn't trust you," he told Louie.

Louie looked around. So far as he could tell, they were still alone. Except for the statue, lying on its back, and he didn't think that was who Froome meant.

"Who doesn't?" he asked.

"Father."

Louie nodded, still looking around them.

"Who's invisible?" he asked.

Froome glared at him, the lantern's light giving his eyes a wicked glow. Or had that glow been there all along and he'd just managed to not notice it? Because other things were changing with Froome. He didn't seem quite so *human* anymore.

"You're another spy!" Froome cried.

He lunged for Louie, but Louie had been expecting something like that and was already in motion. He darted around the table and grabbed the lantern. The texture was horrible—like holding something alive instead of metal and glass. And that stupid mummified hand still clung to the handle.

"Back off," he warned, "or I break this."

He was planning to do it anyway, since that was what the statue had seemed to be trying to tell him, and whatever else the statue was, at least it looked human. But he was hoping to find a way to do it that would also give himself a chance to escape.

"You'll set them all free, will you?" Froome asked. He didn't try to grab Louie. Instead, he stood there now, smiling. "All those poor trapped souls. Did they tell you you'd be a hero?"

Louie caught movement from the corner of his eyes. He looked away for a moment to see that dozens of little pumpkin-bodied men and women were filling the park, all moving toward the stone table. He returned his attention to Froome.

"I'm no hero," he said.

"Oh, that's obvious, kid."

"But I will break this."

"Go ahead."

Great, Louie thought. He looked at the rest of the junk on the stone tabletop. There was probably something else he was supposed to break, but how was he supposed to figure out what it was? It was all just weird-ass crap.

He supposed that the fleshy feel of the lantern should have been a giveaway. It probably wouldn't break even if he threw it against the table.

What he did know was that just holding it was giving him a serious case of the creeps.

"What makes you think you're the good guy, anyway?" Froome asked him.

The others were close now, too close. They stayed maybe ten, twelve feet back, but they made a circle about seven people deep and growing.

"Why is what we're doing here automatically evil?" Froome went on. "I told you no lies. The ones who were changed did so of their own free will. No one was forced. No evil army is being amassed. We are simply making unhappy lives content. Holding out the hand of friendship to those who have nothing. Who have less than nothing."

At the words "free will," Louie remembered Froome's odd reaction earlier when the business of favours had come up.

"Then what's the deal with that statue?" he asked. "Who made it? Who's it supposed to be and what do you have against the guy?"

"That's none of your business."

"Remember that chocolate bar and the favour you say you owe me?" Froome glowered at him. "What of it?"

"Do me a favour," Louie said, "and explain the statue to me."

An unhappy murmur arose from the crowd around them.

"You're all the same," Froome said. "Meddlers who all think you know what's better for us than we do."

"Hey," Louie said. "I know all about that kind of thing. Up above, I've always got somebody trying to fix my life for me. They think they know best, but I don't buy it."

"Then you should be sympathetic to us."

"I never said I wasn't. It's just—what's the deal with the statue? I put my hand on it and it talked to me. You know, in my head. It asked me for help."

"So of course you would give it to them, the meddlers, rather than stand with us."

Them? Louie thought, glancing at the statue. There was only one figure lying there. Did this crazy little guy think that the man the statue was based on had a bird, and the bird was after him, too? Hello, paranoid much?

"So this is a statue of someone who was spying on you?" he asked.

"They weren't always statues," Froome told him. "Father turned them to stone."

"Whoa. People don't just get turned into stone."

"No? But they can give up their soul's light and change from human to us? And statues can speak to you in your head. How is the one any less possible than the other?"

"It's just…"

His voice trailed off. He realized two things. The first was…

"Yes," Froome said. "Father thinks you'll make a fine statue."

And the second was, that maybe the statue hadn't meant for him to break the lantern. Unless Froome was a better player than Louie thought he was, Froome really didn't care if the lantern was broken or not. So maybe the statue had been trying to tell him to break the contact between the lantern and the mummified hand. Because of all the weird things on that stone table, the withered hand clutching the lantern's handle was definitely the weirdest.

So he grabbed at it with his free hand.

He was almost too late. He could feel an impossible weight spreading through his limbs. Flesh turning to stone, bowing him down.

But he was able to grasp the hand.

And almost jerked his hand away when it began to wriggle in his grip.

But he held on. He ripped it away from the handle.

And was blinded by the flare of light that burst from the lantern.

He dropped the lantern, but managed to keep his grip on the squirming, mummified hand. Blinded, he stumbled against the stone table, his body still feeling heavy…so heavy…

He heard the crowd wailing. Froome screeching.

And then he heard the sound of a harp and he figured he'd died and somehow managed to luck his way into Heaven, because where else did you hear harps?

"I am not happy," a deep, resonating voice said.

Uh-oh, Louie thought. They figured out that I'm not supposed to be here in Heaven.

He cracked his eyes open and pushed himself upright from the table. He was still holding the hand, but it was limp in his grip now. He saw Froome, trembling with fear. The crowd was backing away.

From him?

No, he realized. From something behind him. He turned to see two men standing where the statue had been. One looked just like the statue, a tall, white guy with long hair and thin beard. The other was a bald black man and maybe the biggest person Louie had ever seen.

He could still hear the harp playing, but couldn't see where it was coming from, or who was playing it.

"What will we do with them?" the guy who'd been the statue said.

"Teach them a lesson," the black man said. "Meddling, were we? Let them see what true meddling is."

"Wait a sec'," Louie said.

He held up his hand to get their attention, realized it was the one with the mummified hand, and brought it quickly down again. But it had gotten the result. The two men were both looking at him.

"We haven't forgotten the debt we owe you," the black man said. "But let us deal with these vermin first."

Louie swallowed. This was all so not his business, except he'd made it his business, hadn't he?

"It's about your dealing with them," he said.

"What are you trying to say?" the black man's companion asked.

When Louie turned his attention to him, he saw that the guy's fingers were moving at his sides, moving in the same tempo as the harping.

"Well, they didn't do anything wrong," Louie said.

"They turned us into stone."

"And stole the souls of the helpless," the black man added.

"Well, yeah," Louie said. "They turned you into stone. But that's only because you were interfering. Nobody's soul got stolen. They all chose to be changed."

The harper—Louie had to think of him as that, the way his fingers called up harp music from the air—shook his head.

"They preyed on the hopeless and the helpless," he said. "People too far gone to make a decision on their own."

"How do you know?" Louie asked. "Have you been where they were?"

"No, but I—"

"And what makes the life they'd have here so much worse than what they had before?"

Louie was thinking of Froome, the look on his face when he said the people who came to them provided company.

"They're part of a community down here," he went on. "They're looking after each other. So they're not human—so what? I'm getting the idea that neither of you are either. But tell me this: what gives you the right to decide what they should or shouldn't be?"

There was a long moment of silence.

"They still attacked us for no reason," the black man finally said.

"Is that true?" Louie asked Froome.

The little guy still looked scared, but Louie's defense seemed to be giving him some courage.

"Technically, I suppose they're right, kid," he said. "But they've been down here before—if not them, then their kind. Big old powerful spirits who decide how things are going to be. Father knew that if we didn't take them by surprise, then we'd be helpless before them."

"You keep saying 'father'," Louie said. "Where is he?"

"You're holding all that's left of him in this world. He can only be with us when he holds da slockit light. Then he has the power to change one thing into another. We knew there'd be problems when we found the lantern and put the two of them together, but the chance to make things a little better down here seemed worth it."

Louie turned back to the harper and his companion.

"Are you seeing what I am here?" he asked.

Both men shook their heads.

"Well, I think it's pretty obvious," Louie said. "You came down here, with your minds made up that Froome and his people are all evil, and they assumed the worst of you as well. Sort of like willful misunderstandings—because I guess all of you have history, am I right? Seems to me, the best thing for everybody is for us to go back where we came from and leave the people down here alone to mind their own business."

The black man frowned, but the harper gave a slow nod.

"He's right, Lucius," he told his companion.

Lucius nodded. "I know. But it rankles."

"So can I give this back?" Louie asked, holding up the hand.

The harper's gaze went to Froome. "And when Father has his power back?"

"You go free," Froome said. "You have my word on that. Just as you have my word that no one joins us except of their own free will."

"The word of a goblin," Lucius muttered.

"But no less his word," the harper said. "Except you don't rule down here, do you? Goonasekara is your king."

"Not anymore. Cornig Fairnswanter holds that title—or at least we let him think he does. Our true king is Father, who returned to us from beyond the grave in our time of need."

"And do we have his word?"

Froome nodded. "I can speak for him. The real question is, do we have your word that we will be left alone?"

The harper stilled the movement of his fingers and the music faded. "You have our word," he said.

Louie walked over to Froome and gave him the hand.

"No hard feelings, right?" he said.

"None at all. They would have kept coming and we would have ended up with a park full of statues until one of them finally got through our defenses and destroyed our world."

Louie blinked at him. "Uh, right. Whatever."

He started to turn, but Froome held out a hand.

"I meant, thank you," he said as he and Louie shook.

Louie paused and looked at the debris on the stone table.

"Hey, can I have this?" he asked, picking up a small shiny object.

"Of course."

"Thanks."

When he turned, the crowd parted, making an avenue for him and the two men to walk down.

"What brought you here?" the harper asked Louie once they'd left the crowd behind.

"This woman named Marion asked me to scout things out for her. Either one of you her husband?"

"If you mean Meran, then that would be me," the harper said. He smiled and elbowed Lucius. "Trust her to be bring the voice of reason even into Goblinburg."

"We did let things get out of hand," Lucius said.

"But we had to be careful," the harper said. "We couldn't just walk in and demand an answer."

Lucius nodded. "We had no choice. We had to scout things out first."

Walking beside them, Louie smiled to himself. They might be these old powerful spirits, but right now they just sounded like they were working up their excuses for when they had to tell Meran how things had gotten so out of hand.

"Here," Louie said. "I brought you something."

He'd come to the big house on Stanton Street at the insistence of his companions, but he hadn't wanted to go in, so Meran had come out onto the porch to thank him. He opened his hand now and offered her the sliver of mica that he'd taken from the stone table.

"It's for that weird-ass wallet of yours," he said.

Meran smiled. "It's perfect," she said. "Thank you."

Louie blushed, then blushed more when she leaned forward and kissed his cheek.

"Can I ask you something?" Louie asked.

"Of course."

"Why'd you come to me? I saw those guys in Jimmy's. I bet any one of them would have done it for you."

She nodded. "But I needed someone human."

Louie blinked. "So what? You're telling me they're not?"

"Not everything is what it appears," she said.

"You're telling me. I guess you don't know any actual, um, humans, right?"

Meran laughed. "I know hundreds."

"So when you asked me..."

"I suppose there are others I could have asked," she said, "but I knew you could do it. And I was right. You did it and more."

"I guess. Do you think people will leave them alone—the ones that choose to stay below and be...um..."

"Goblins?"

"Is that what they are?"

"Pretty much."

"So will they?" Louie asked.

"I know Cerin and Lucius will," Meran told him.

She reached into her pocket and pulled out some money.

"No, it's okay," Louie said. "I didn't do it for the money—not in the end."

"Will you at least come back to visit? The house isn't always full of the noise and confusion you see here today."

"Don't take this wrong," Louie told her, "but I'm like those goblins down below. I don't want to be anybody's salvage project."

"How about being somebody's friend?"

Louie looked at her for a long moment. He didn't see that look in her eyes, the weighing of the damage, the deciding how much work it would take to fix up the poor little kid he looked to be.

"Yeah," he said, dropping his gaze to the ground. "I guess I could do that."

"Don't think I won't hold you to it," she said.

# The World
# in a Box

Somewhere in the world there is a box, and if you open that box, inside it you'll find the world.

What does that mean? I don't know. I think it's like one of those Zen riddles that you're not really supposed to figure out. It's just supposed to make you think—you know, the whole *it's the journey that's important* thing, not the destination.

I can't even remember where I heard it. It was probably one of those late night, slight inebriated conversations you can get into, especially when you're young and weighing in on all the great mysteries of the universe. Like, why are we here and where do we go when we die? Or, what if this world is all a dream and one of us is the dreamer? Or, do things exist only because we expect them to?

Man, if I knew now what I thought I did then, I'd be a very wise man.

Looking back, you have to smile. The meaning of life. Omnipotent dreamers. The world hidden in a box.

Except one day I found that box.

I was working part-time at the Antique Market Mall, looking after my downstairs neighbour Lizzie's booth in the weekday afternoons so that she could stay home with her two daughters and not have to pay for a babysitter. Money was tight. Money's always tight, but it was a little more so than usual that December.

As a musician, I work evenings anyway—when I have a gig—so it was no big deal for me to help out. I just didn't want to have to get up too early in the morning. There are limits to what we'll do for our friends. I could have stayed home and taken on the role of babysitter, but much as I like her kids, after ten minutes I run out of ways to amuse them. And they *don't* amuse themselves. Trust me. I found that out the hard way.

They're great when Lizzie's around, but when she's not, they can sense my general helplessness and act like their attention spans are only three seconds long. I know that's not true. When Lizzie's at home, it's at least five minutes.

So anyway, I look after the booth.

It's not hard work. Because I don't own it, I don't have to worry about prettying up the displays or where I'm going to get new stock. I just go in with a book and catch up on my reading, or wander around some of the nearby booths and shoot the breeze with whoever's working that day while I keep an eye on Lizzie's space.

She believes the stuff should sell itself—she prides herself on her merchandise and even claims the coolest stuff somehow appears to find her— so I'm not expected to pitch her wares. I wouldn't be much good at it anyway since her stock is mostly vintage clothing, jewellery and collectibles. What do I know about any of that beyond what I've learned helping her out? Now, if she were selling vintage guitars, that'd be a whole other story.

My favourite customers are the teenage girls and the twenty-somethings because they just get so excited about finding this top or that necklace. When they come in two or three at a time, their enthusiasm ricochets off each other until they get totally giddy and you can't help smiling with them.

My least favourite are out-of-town dealers or the local "experts" that you also run into at every garage sale, church bazaar or flea market. They just know too much, are more than willing to share that knowledge at great length, and always expect some impossible deal that I can't give them and Lizzie shouldn't.

But a customer's a customer, so I smile and am polite to all of them, even the ones that need a bang on the ear. Because it's Lizzie's rep that's under scrutiny here, not mine.

People often wonder if Lizzie and I are a couple, but really we're just friends who like to hang out together. Sometimes it's easier to do things with a friendly neighbour, than to try to work your way through the morass of the dating scene. You'd think a musician would have a better chance at hooking up with someone than most, but you'd be wrong. And as a single, working mom, Lizzie often says that she simply doesn't have time to play the whole dating game, just saying she ever found a guy that wasn't a jerk, "present company excepted," she'll add to me.

She doesn't have to. I can be as much of an idiot as the next guy. But I try not to be mean. You know, set up false expectations, or treat somebody crappy just because it's not working out.

Maybe Lizzie and I are just lazy, but it's kind of nice to be able to rent a DVD on a night off and have someone to watch it with. Or to share a dinner because, let's face it—in my case—cooking for one sucks. Come my turn, I'm not as adventurous as Lizzie is, but sometimes the tried-and-true works just fine. When I serve up macaroni and cheese, I'm like a hero to Lizzie's girls. And Lizzie, well, she's just happy to have someone else cook, so there are no complaints from her on those nights either.

I suppose the down side is that you get used to how things are going and you stop making any effort to find that real significant other who might be waiting for you somewhere out there in the big old world. Truth is, I don't go looking at all anymore and probably wouldn't know her unless she came up to me wearing a big sign around her neck saying, "It's me, stupid."

It's like what you find on the shelves of the various booths here in the antique mall. Every once in awhile I've gone with Lizzie on her rounds—mostly to keep the girls out of mischief—and I walk by tables of crap where she and the other dealers find treasure. I guess you need the eye for it. It doesn't look like much to me until I see it on a shelf here with a jacked-up price tag on it and then it's, of course, that candelabra is worth fifty bucks. It's gorgeous. But the dealer who bought it at a yard sale found it in a box under a table, nestled in a tangle of wires, and got it for three dollars.

And don't they love to talk about those finds.

But I don't mind. I get a kick out of listening to them go on about their hits and misses and all the arcane knowledge they have about pretty much anything you can think of. It's interesting—if not particularly useful to me otherwise—to learn how to tell the difference between amber and yellow glass, or a true Victorian desk and a 1940s knock-off. But then I've always been a magpie for trivia, not limited to, but particularly the tidbits that are relevant to my own field of reference. Don't get me started on the background of resonator guitars or the original source of some old Tex-Mex tune.

Mind you, the dealers also love to gossip, and that's not so interesting. Everybody in here has something to say about everybody else, but I don't take sides or make alliances. I follow Lizzie's lead and accept everybody at face value, don't make fast friends, and while it's not in my nature to automatically distrust anybody, I keep a healthy dose of skepticism on hand with everyone I meet there.

It was early December when I came across the box in Trevor's booth, which is two over from Lizzie's. It was just a little wooden three-dimensional square with a fitted lid, small enough to nestle in the palm of your hand. Walnut, maybe. Or butternut. I know next to nothing about that kind of thing unless we're talking about the tops of guitars, or neck stocks.

Trevor had a customer, a feisty old woman who also comes by Lizzie's booth regularly, haggling fiercely over every purchase, but never getting obnoxious about it. It was funny seeing the two of them at it. Trevor's a big man, over six feet tall with a lot of weight on his frame, but he doesn't look fat. Just seriously substantial. Big beard and bald head. The top of Grace's head barely reaches Trevor's chin. Small and delicately-boned like a bird, she held her own in the bargaining and had a salty tongue that always made me laugh.

"Oh please," she was saying to him. "Your prices are getting higher than a giraffe's balls."

Trevor tried to keep a straight face. He looked away, turning in my direction where I was already grinning, and then he lost it.

Once we'd all finished laughing, I went back to browsing his shelves and they started bargaining again. That's when I spied the little wooden box, sitting in between an old pair of opera glasses with mother of pearl inlay and a little brass statue of Joan of Arc that was missing the tip of its little sword. I turned the box over in my hands, attracted to it for no reason that I could fathom. I'd like to say that I had a flash of premonition at that moment, a forewarning that my perception of everything was about to change, but the truth is all I felt was a mild curiosity.

The wood had been oiled, bringing out the grain, and the sides had been put together with dove-tail joints—hand-carved ones rather than machined, which meant it was probably from the 1800s and explained the twenty-five dollar price tag. There were no hinges. The lid simply lifted off, which I proceeded to do.

And then it seemed the world went still all around me.

You know those photographs of the earth taken from one of the space shuttles, the ones that show this beautiful green and blue sphere just floating there in the black velvet reaches of outer space? That's what was inside the box—not a photograph, but a tiny replica of the earth floating there in space.

I held it closer to my eye, trying to figure out the illusion. But it wasn't. An illusion, I mean. Impossible as it should be, somehow there really seemed to be a tiny planet hovering there in the middle of the box.

"Pretty little thing, isn't it?"

I almost dropped the box, but I managed to keep my grip on it as I turned to Trevor.

"It's from the 1800s," he said. "Probably a snuff box. Or maybe something to keep stamps in. See this?"

He reached out a hand and reluctantly, I passed the box over to him. I almost had a heart attack when he stuck his finger inside, the better to hold it as he showed me the joints.

"Hand-carved," he said. "And look how snugly the lid still fits on it. I picked it up at an estate sale last week." His gaze lifted to mine. "I could let you have it for twenty."

It was an automatic spiel, but it surprised me because, after my first few days of booth-sitting, nobody in here ever tried to sell me anything because I didn't buy anything. But mostly I couldn't understand how he obviously couldn't—or at least didn't—see the world slowly spinning inside.

He handed it back to me and I looked inside.

The little planet was still there.

"Sure," I found myself saying as I reached into my pocket with my free hand for the money. "I'll take it."

We might have exchanged a few more words, but I don't remember. I just took my purchase back to Lizzie's booth and sat there staring inside it until I realized that Trevor was giving me a puzzled look. Well, I guess it must have seemed weird, me sitting there, mesmerized by the box the way I was.

I caught his gaze before he could turn away and gave him a shrug and a smile. Putting the lid back on, I set it on the counter in front of me.

I desperately wanted to ask him what he saw when he looked inside the box, but managed not to. Obviously, he didn't see anything or he'd have kept it. Or sold it for a lot more than twenty dollars.

Unless I had just imagined it.

I popped the lid and had another quick look.

Still there.

Or I was still imagining it.

I closed the lid again.

But if I wasn't imagining it, then what was it?

Lizzie came in just before closing time with a faux fur coat she'd picked up at the Sally Ann. She was alone, so I assumed the girls were playing with the Rodriguez twins who lived next door to our house.

It must have started snowing again because that thick auburn mane of Lizzie's hair sparkled with melted flakes. She had a rosy flush to her cheeks.

I've never understood why her ex left her and the girls. What could he have been thinking? Lizzie's everything a guy could want in a woman: she's smart, funny, pretty as anything, even-tempered and just a little mischievous. And yes, Sophie and Emaline are a handful, but they're a good-natured, happy handful, not a couple of surly kids. And they do know how to take a time-out.

"How's it been today?" she asked.

"Slow."

"How slow?"

"I sold a twelve-dollar brooch for ten bucks."

She sighed, then shook her head, determined not to let it get her down. The past couple of weeks had been particularly bad. Yesterday she hadn't had even a single sale.

"Oh well," she said. "Everybody says it'll pick up after Christmas."

I nodded. Apparently, people didn't buy used goods to give as presents—even if they were high-priced and classy like what you could find here in the antique mall.

"What do you have there?" she asked.

"Just a little box I got from Trevor."

She grinned. "Don't tell me you're finally getting the fever."

"Hardly." I handed it over to her so she could have a look at it. "I just liked it."

I realized I was holding my breath as she turned it over in her hands and then opened it.

"It's pretty," she said. "You can use it to hold your guitar picks."

I nodded, trying not to show my disappointment. I'd wanted her to see the planet, too. It would have, oh I don't know, been this little shared secret known only to the two of us, and I'd have liked that. Instead, I'd just paid twenty dollars for an admittedly pretty little box in which I imagined I could see a piece of magic.

"What's the matter?" Lizzie asked. "You have the funniest look on your face."

"It's nothing. I guess I just overpaid Trevor for it."

"How much was it?"

"Twenty-five. But he gave it to me for twenty."

Lizzie shook her head. "Well, it is very pretty…"

"And it's from the 1800s," I said, adding silently to myself, not to mention that it holds the illusion of a miniature earth floating in space.

"He'd probably take it back if you asked. Do you want me to?"

"No," I said as she returned the box to me. "I still like it. And I do need something to keep my picks in."

I peeked inside. The planet was still there.

I didn't have a gig that night, but Lizzie actually had a date with this guy she'd met at her friend Cathy's café earlier in the day.

"I'm as surprised as you that I said yes," she said as we walked home from the antique mall. "But he seemed nice and what the heck, right? I can't let myself turn into a complete spinster."

"You'd never be a spinster," I told her.

The girls were sleeping overnight at the twins' house next door, so once I heard Lizzie's front door close downstairs, I knew the building was empty except for myself. Mine's the smaller of the two apartments that make up the house because the ground floor has an extra bedroom tacked on at the back. But I have plenty of room since I only have myself and my instruments to worry about. I love to read, but I don't keep books when I'm done. Instead, I trade them back in at the secondhand shop and get a bunch of new ones.

My gear—that's another story. I can't seem to let a guitar or an amp, or even a pedal, leave my possession, but I can't stop picking up new ones, either. Mostly used, because like a guy I used to play with once said, "The only thing a guitarist should buy new are strings and picks." There's something to be said about an instrument that's got a little history to it, no question. But you get enough of them and they really start to fill up the place. Lizzie says my apartment looks like an instrument shop, except nothing's for sale.

What can I say? It's true.

I opened a can of pea soup and put it on the stove to warm. No shared meal tonight because Lizzie was eating out with her date. While I waited for the soup to heat up, I took the box out of my pocket and removed the lid. The miniature version of the earth was still floating inside.

This must be how God sees the world, I thought as I looked down on it.

I got so caught up in staring at it that my soup almost boiled over.

I had flying dreams that night.

Not the kind I've had before, where I'm skimming over the rooftops and trees and lamp posts, looking down on the city below, but it's all close enough to make out details. In these dreams I was floating somewhere in space, out among the stars, and the earth was far, far below me, a sphere of blues and greens the size of a marble because of my perspective. It was so tiny. Like the world in the box I'd bought from Trevor.

That's all I did. I just floated there, looking down at it.

When I woke, I couldn't remember having had a more restful night.

Later that morning I sat at my kitchen table, nursing a coffee and staring out at the snowy streets while I tried to remember where I'd first run across the odd concept of the world in a box. The memory took awhile to come back to me. It was when I was touring with Jenny Wray, back in her cowpunk phase. She does cabaret now with a jazz combo—piano, bass and drums. She decided she only wanted the trio when she made the switch from her country show, so she had to let me go, no hard feelings.

I didn't have any. You could run out of gigs quickly if you burned your bridges every time things didn't go the way you wanted them to. But I'd liked playing with her. For one thing, she was a great person to spend time with on the road. For another, any excuse to bring out my lap steel was good enough for me. I can never get enough country gigs.

That's what I do: I'm a sideman. I had ambitions once of fronting a band, writing my own music, singing my own songs, but I don't have what it takes. I have nothing to say, or at least nothing that I can put in lyrics and music that a hundred others writers haven't already done, and done better. And I don't have the presence, the charisma to be the front man.

I can sing good harmony and play pretty much any style of guitar you want. Electric, acoustic. Blues, rock, folk, country and even a little of that Nouveau Flamenco, but I'm mostly faking the Latin stuff. I have the theory and chops for flamenco, but I don't have the feel. I could never get the rhythms for Celtic music either, but I'm more of a lead player anyway.

Gigging with Jenny, I pretty much got to exercise all my enthusiasms, but especially the country. And Jenny was a blast to play with. Smart, funny, and deadly serious about her music, even when she was doing that goofy cowpunk stuff which was sort of like the Clash channeling Tammy Wynette. She treated her sidemen with respect—which is rarer than you might think in this business. Doesn't make much sense not to, because a lot of the time we're what make the singers sound as good as they do. But there are a lot of divas out there. Though maybe I'm just biased.

I knew Jenny was in town from seeing her face looking back at me from flyers on various telephone poles and the like, advertising an upcoming gig, so I tried calling her at the apartment she still keeps in the city.

We spent awhile catching up before I brought up the whole business with the world in a box.

She laughed. "God, you don't forget anything, do you?"

"Well, it was a weird story—the kind of thing that stays with you."

"I guess."

"I was wondering where you first heard about it."

I could sense her smiling on the other end of the line. "You mean what wise man, hidden far away from the eyes of the world, first revealed these great truths to me?"

I laughed. "Something like that."

"I made it up," she said.

I was holding the box and looked down into it at the earth floating there, suspended in the center of the space in a way that just didn't seem possible, but it was happening all the same.

"Did you now," I said.

"Um-hmm. I was working up a song, actually. Something along the lines of the microcosm reflecting the macrocosm—you know, above as it is below—but it never quite jelled for me. See, I thought of it as being this talisman that allowed whoever had it the ability to make anything happen. They'd be like a God. But then I realized that anyone who did have a talisman that powerful, well then, they probably were God, and it's hard to lay any real doubt or angst on God, you know? His followers can have a crisis of faith, sure. But God? I figure even if He didn't know the answers, He'd let on that He did."

"And being God," I put in, "so it would come to pass."

She laughed. "Something like that. Why are you so interested in this, anyway?"

"Oh, I don't know," I lied. "It's just one of those things that came into my head like an advertising jingle and I haven't been able to get it out again."

"I hate when that happens. Especially when you're sitting down to write something yourself and all you've got in your head is some cheesy oom-pah-pah ditty from a used car lot."

"It wasn't quite that bad," I told her. "Besides, it gave me an excuse to give you a call."

"Now you need an excuse?"

"You know what I mean."

"Sadly, I do," she said. "Where *does* all the time go? I keep meaning to look up friends whenever I get back to town, but it seems like no sooner do I open the door of my apartment, than I'm already packing my bags and hitting the road again without having made one call."

"The price of success."

"Of steady work anyway. Are you coming to the show on Saturday? I can put your name on the guest list."

We talked a little more, then finally said our goodbyes with promises to get together soon.

It had started to snow again while I was on the phone, which was a good thing. It's always a trade off in the winter. When you get a clear, sunny day, it's usually bitter cold. Snow brings its own challenges, but at least you're not freezing your butt off when you venture outdoors and I had to walk to the antique mall soon. And I don't mind shovelling because all we've got is the porch and the walkway to the street.

I looked away from the window and studied the box some more, thinking of what Jenny had said.

The person holding it could make anything happen.

Okay, so it was just an idea she came up with for a song that never went anywhere, but it was in my hand now, as real as the kitchen around me, even if I was the only one who could see it.

Maybe I was making it happen. Maybe I was crazy. But there was one way to find out.

Anything, I thought.

I picked something small.

It had been dead in the antique market for a couple weeks now. None of the dealers were doing well, but poor Lizzie seemed particularly hard hit. I don't think she'd grossed more than forty dollars so far this week and it was already Wednesday.

So let her have a good day, I told the world, floating there in the wooden box I held in my hand.

Let her have an amazing day.

I got to the booth just before one o'clock when I was supposed to take over from her and it was…it was just weird. She had three or four people trying to give her money for stuff they'd already chosen to buy, with another couple looking in the display cabinet with the really pricey jewellery.

When she looked up and caught my eye, I could see the relief in her eyes.

"Thank God you're here," she said. "It's been crazy all morning."

I stuffed my coat under one of the tables and started taking money, wrapping up purchases, and generally making myself useful. It was like when Lizzie did the weekend shows, before she got the booth here. Those one-off shows had always been so successful that it had seemed like a no-brainer to get a permanent place to sell her stuff.

It hadn't been bad the first few months, but this recent run of bad luck had been making her seriously reconsider the feasibility of keeping the booth.

Closing wasn't even a consideration today.

It didn't quiet down until past three, and even then there was never a time when there wasn't somebody looking at the clothing racks or peering into the display cabinets. Lizzie'd had to phone the twins' mother and ask her to pick up the girls from school because she couldn't possibly have gotten away to do it herself.

"Wow," she said. "I guess Peter really did bring me good luck."

"Peter?"

"Peter Hendel—my date from last night. The last thing he said after he kissed me goodnight was, 'That one's to bring you luck tomorrow,' which made me feel a little bad because I guess I was going on a bit too much about how lousy business has been."

No, I wanted to tell her. I brought you this luck—me and the world in my little wooden box that no one can see.

Because don't think I hadn't been thinking about it as we dealt with the press of people wanting to buy things. I'd made the wish, and it had come true, just like that. What made it really obvious was how we were the only booth in the mall doing such a bang-up trade today.

I wasn't about to tell Lizzie that, but it annoyed me that this Peter guy was getting the credit for it, just as it annoyed me more when she went on to tell me what a great time she'd had on her date. I don't know why that was. It's not like she hasn't gone out with other guys since I've known her, and it never bothered me those times. We don't have some kind of *When Harry Met Sally* thing happening here—you know, we're right for each other but we just don't know it.

Okay, I'm lying. I'm crazy about her and I know she doesn't feel the same way about me. I haven't exactly asked her, but you pick up on these things and, while I can tell she likes me really well as a friend, I don't get the feeling she's ever considered me in any other light. I've had enough women come on to me at gigs to know when someone's attracted to you, and Lizzie doesn't even flirt with me, so there you go.

But I was good with it. At least, that's what I've always told myself. Except there was something about the sparkle in her eye when she was talking about this guy, not to mention the way he'd stolen my thunder with his damned "good luck kiss," that just ticked me off today. Ticked me off enough that I found myself in a cubicle in the washroom with the box open in my hand saying something along the lines of how whatever else might happen, a relationship with Peter just wasn't going to work out. It wasn't even going to get started.

Okay, I'm not exactly proud of doing it. But it's not like I tried to work up some mojo to make Lizzie want me instead. And even with the increased business at the booth, and that weird little phenomenon of the world suspended in its wooden box, I hadn't totally bought into the magic being real anyway.

But Peter never called Lizzie like he'd promised he would.

By Friday it was still so busy at Lizzie's booth that we were both working there. We'd probably been in each other's company more in the past few days than we ever had—two full days at the booth, sharing dinner and pricing stock in the evenings. It was lucky that I didn't have a gig either night so I could help out, though I did have one tonight.

Our being together hadn't been like some romantic thing. We were both too busy trying to get everything done. The girls were great, helping out where they could, amusing themselves and keeping out of the way when they couldn't.

But we weren't so busy that I didn't notice Lizzie getting more and more depressed and it didn't take any great genius to figure out why.

"I don't get it," she said as we were restocking her booth before opening on Friday morning. "We hit it off amazingly well, so why hasn't he called like he said he would?"

She looked at me like I had the answer.

And of course I did. But it was the last thing I could tell her.

"Maybe he just got called away on business," I said.

"I suppose. But they don't have phones where he had to go? I hate it when people promise they're going to do something and then they don't. It makes me feel so pathetic, eagerly awaiting some stupid phone call that's never going to come."

I could have gotten mad at Peter for treating her so bad, but it wasn't his fault, was it?

Truth is, this magic business was trickier than I thought. What I hadn't realized was the whole concept of cause and effect that came into play when you used it. It seemed that if you made something happen in one place, then it took away the possibility of it happening elsewhere. Like all these people buying stuff from Lizzie. Because I'd made them come to her, nobody was shopping at the other booths and you could feel the resentment from the other dealers. Or by keeping Peter away from Lizzie. All I'd done was leave her feeling progressively more miserable—even with all her recent financial success in the past few days.

I excused myself before the store opened and went back to the wash-room. I told the world in its box to let whatever was going to happen between Peter and Lizzie play itself out. And to tone down the buying frenzy.

If I hadn't believed that the magic worked before, I had to now.

When the doors opened, there was no rush like there had been the past few days. And it stayed relatively quiet throughout the day. But even though our sales had died down, everybody else's picked up.

And then just around noon, this good-looking guy came up to the booth with a sheepish look and a bouquet of roses. I didn't have to ask if it was Peter. All I had to do was look at Lizzie's face as he made his apologies. The booth was so small that I couldn't help but overhear what he was saying.

His mom had fallen sick. Flew out immediately to see her. No chance to call, everything was so crazy. Just got back this morning. Yes, she was fine now. A false alarm, thank God.

No, thank me, I thought.

"It's pretty quiet," I told Lizzie. "Why don't you guys go have some lunch or something."

Her beaming smile made me feel even smaller for what I'd done.

"I owe you one," she said.

"You don't owe me a thing," I told her. "Go have some fun."

I watched them walk away, then turned to help a customer who was hemming and hawing over whether to buy a five-dollar brooch.

Yup, things had changed, all right.

My gig didn't go so well that night. The singer who'd hired us kept straying from the set list of stuff we'd worked on, which wasn't a huge problem. The musicians were all professionals. We could keep up. But the music didn't sound tight like it had in rehearsal, and when the singer started to give us a hard time about it after the first set, I wanted to whack him on the head with my guitar.

Or maybe speak a few words into the wooden box that was in the pock-et of my winter coat draped across my gear bag on the side of the stage.

But I did neither. The band soldiered on and the gig came to an end the way every gig does, the good ones and the bad ones. We got paid and I went home.

I was surprised to see the lights on in Lizzie's place.

I tried to be quiet, but it's hard with a guitar case, amplifier and gig bag of cables and pedals. I was on the landing, halfway up the stairs, when I heard Lizzie's door open.

"Sorry," I started to say.

I didn't finish. Lizzie was crying and her face looked bruised.

I left my gear on the landing and hurried back down the stairs. She looked worse up close. Black eye, with a cut on the brow above it. A bruised cheek. Her lips were swollen, the lower one split.

"God, Lizzie! What happened?"

"I…I don't even know for sure…"

She let me steer her back into her apartment. Luckily the kids were next door—they were going to think they lived there pretty soon. I sat Lizzie at the kitchen table, then put a kettle on and took a box of herbal tea down from the cupboard. My hands were shaking as I got a couple of teabags out and rinsed the teapot with hot water.

"Who did this to you?" I asked her because I was going to kill whoever had done it.

"It…it was Peter," she said.

My anger deflated into a sick guilt.

Peter.

Oh, God. *I'd* done this to her, or I might as well have, because I'd worked the little mojo with my world in a box that had brought him back to her this afternoon.

The water started to boil. I emptied the teapot, dropped the teabags in and poured the boiling water over them. Covering it with a cozy, I brought it and a couple of mugs to the table.

"Do you want to talk about it?" I asked.

She shook her head and just reached a hand across the table. I hesitated a moment, then took her hand, stroking the top of it in helpless comfort. I don't know how long we sat there, but after awhile she began to tell me what happened.

They'd gone for lunch, were just hitting it off so well. They came back here, put the roses in water and made arrangements for the girls to stay next door. Then it was off to dinner, followed by what was supposed to be just a few drinks at a jazz bar, except Peter had gone way over any acceptable limit.

"I was a little tipsy, too," she said. "Enough that I knew we should be taking a cab from the club. But he insisted he was fine to drive. Said he'd been drinking water as well, though I don't remember that. I don't know why I got into that car with him. I just didn't want him to think I was pushy, I guess, and how stupid was that?

"Anyway, he lost control running a red light and the next thing I knew we were smashing into a parked car—which is how I got my lovely new facial. I look like the Frankenstein monster."

"You couldn't look ugly if you tried," I told her.

She shook her head. "You always have something nice to say, don't you?"

Maybe not, because right then I didn't have a single response. When she fell silent, I poured tea for us one-handedly. She gave me the sense that she was never going to let go of my other hand. That it was her only anchor to the normal world.

"When you first said Peter'd done this to you, I thought..." I began, but then let my voice trail off.

But she picked up on where I'd been going with that.

"Oh, God. That would have been even more horrible. It's bad enough that he had such disregard for our lives. And what if he'd hit somebody?" She shook her head. "Well, I won't be seeing him again, unless it goes to court and I'm asked to testify and you can bet I'll tell the whole truth."

I nodded. I hated drunk drivers. One of my friends had been killed by one back when I was in high school. So far as I was concerned, there was no excuse to get behind the wheel if you were over the limit. Better yet, if you were planning to drive, abstain completely. But some people didn't see it that way. It was all trying to get one past the police, with no consideration for the innocent people that might be hurt.

After a time, Lizzie got tired enough that I could put her to bed. I just took off her shoes and got her to stretch out on her bed, then covered her up with a blanket. She caught my arm before I could go.

"Could you...don't leave me alone..."

"I won't," I told her. "I'll make up a bed for myself on the couch. I just need to get my gear out of the hall first."

She fell asleep at my promise and didn't hear the rest of what I'd said.

144

I slipped out of the bedroom and brought my guitar and gear up to my apartment. It took me only a couple of minutes and then I was back in her place. I closed the door and checked in on her. She was still sleeping. I picked up my coat from where I'd dropped it coming into the apartment earlier. Taking the wooden box out of its pocket, I went and sat down on the couch.

I tried to compose myself, but all I could think of was how that man had endangered Lizzie.

Peter Hendel.

Peter Hendel needed some serious Old Testament eye for an eye, something to hurt him as much as he'd hurt Lizzie, and I was just the guy to bring it down upon him in Biblical proportions. I had the means, right here in my hands. And I had the will.

The trouble was, every time I'd done something with the world in its wooden box, it had gone wrong.

I knew why, too.

I was because I wasn't omnipotent. I couldn't see all the ramifications of even the simplest wish.

And maybe that was the problem. Not just that I couldn't see how making one thing happen would cause unforeseen consequences. I'd been thinking in terms of wishes.

The world didn't work on wishes. There were no free rides.

I'd been generous at first. Helping Lizzie with her slumping sales. But that had taken prosperity from others.

Then I'd been selfish and that had only resulted in making Lizzie miserable.

So I tried to do the right thing, and that had made things even worse.

I had the feeling it would always work out like that.

I could bring rains to some drought-stricken part of the world, but it would only take that rain away from somewhere else and perhaps cause a worse drought there.

I could try to bring peace to parts of the world where there was war. I could stop all the car bombings and acts of terrorism. But bottling it all up would probably make it explode even worse somewhere else.

And right here, on a more personal level, I could bring retribution to Peter Hendel—and God, did I want to—but what ramifications would that have elsewhere in the world?

The box was open in my hand and I had been staring at the small sphere suspended there inside it as all of this was going through my head.

Slowly, I took the lid and put it back on.

Wishes and magic weren't a solution.

I don't know that there are ever real solutions to anything. Not easy ones, at any rate. Mostly, we just seem to muddle through our lives, and maybe that's what we're supposed to do. Learn what we can as we live our lives and make sure that we bring what goodness we can into the world at our individual level as we try to win back the darkness one little bit at a time.

The journey, not the destination.

I moved the box back and forth from one hand to another.

So maybe I'd learned something from this, but I'll tell you now, I wish I'd never found the damn thing.

And what was I supposed to do with it now?

What Lizzie really needed to help her heal was her girls. They were what would remind her that there was still light in the world. They were the best reason to be brave and to carry on that I could think of. She gave a slow nod in agreement and the first touch of a smile since she'd called to me in the hall last night.

We told them that their mom had been in a car accident and left it at that. I went in to work the booth so that Lizzie could have the day with them and wouldn't have to endure the gossip of all the dealers as they checked out her bruises and cuts.

When the antique market closed at the end of an average day of sales, I went to the club where Jenny was playing and got lucky because they were just finishing their sound check. After exchanging hellos with her band, Jenny and I went and sat at the bar to have a coffee. She never drinks before a show and I wasn't in the mood for a beer—not with Lizzie's story still fresh in my mind. Jenny was still in jeans and a sweater, her straight blonde hair tied back in a ponytail. It made her look younger than I knew she was. Tonight, at the show, she'd be wearing the heels and black cocktail dress, her hair pinned up in a loose coil, her make-up just right.

I took out the box and put it on the bar in front of her.

"What's this?" she said.

"The world in a box."

She laughed. "Really?"

"If you want it to be."

"My, aren't you being mysterious."

She picked up the box and admired it for a moment before taking off the lid and looking inside.

"There's no world," she said.

"Then I guess you'll need to find one to put in it."

I was relieved. So she didn't see it either. I don't know why I could and no one else, but I didn't want the responsibility of taking care of it anymore. I also didn't want it to fall into the wrong hands—which were those belonging to anyone who could see that little earth suspended inside, I'd decided.

Jenny was a safe bet. She was sentimental and would keep it safe. And since she couldn't see the world, everything else would be safe, too. Or at least as safe as things can be in a world where wishes actually work.

"Are you staying for the show?" she asked.

I shook my head. Lizzie had called before I left the antique mall, asking if I wanted to come over for dinner and a movie tonight. There had been something different in her voice. Not the understandable anxiety I'd heard last night. Not the sadness from last week, either, or even a promise. Just something different. Maybe I was only imagining it.

But when I heard her voice I realized that I needed to depend even less on wishes and what-ifs than I had before I found the box. I had to make an effort so that the days to come might go the way I wanted them to, because they weren't just going to come to me.

I had a journey to take, after all.

And I didn't want to take it alone.

# *This Moment*

*I* reached under the counter for my camera as soon as I saw the bear coming up the sidewalk. Its rolling gait took it right alongside the cast iron rails of the patio, where a half dozen customers sat oblivious to its presence, and I thought the unusual sight warranted documentation. It's weird enough to see a bear downtown in the late afternoon, but this one had what appeared to be either a little man or an otter riding on its back. I'm not sure which, but he was definitely wearing clothes—probably buckskins, fancied up with beadwork and dangling fringes of coloured I'm-not-sure-what. Strips of cloth, maybe. Or yarn.

I managed to get off a couple of good shots before the bear ambled out of range, then I pressed my face against the plate glass and watched them until they were lost to sight. Straightening from the window, I switched my camera to its monitor function and checked its small LCD screen.

They weren't in either shot—neither the bear, nor its jaunty rider. There was only the outside patio with the street behind it.

I wasn't particularly surprised. While I could see these sorts of things on the camera's display screen when I took the picture, they never showed up in playback. It was as though they disappeared into some digital limbo between the one moment and the next, though the more logical explanation was that they hadn't been there at all. I'd think that I was imagining these sightings, but sometimes I could bring up a hint of the missing subject on my computer screen. I'd play around in Photoshop with various image adjustment modes until finally a pixilated ghost hovered there, faint, but discernable.

And at that point, anyone could see it. Or at least that ghost of it I had managed to bring into view.

"Cool," Andrew said, when he saw one of them on my computer screen a few months ago. "How'd you get that effect?"

I'd only shrugged, not even trying for an explanation.

"Could you do me a unicorn, Tom? With ocean waves for a background?"

Andrew used to be a linebacker in high school, but he has a thing for unicorns. Don't ask.

"I don't even know how I did this one," I lied.

"But if you figure it out..."

I'd nodded. "You'll be the first in line to get one."

I had a whole collection of shots taken through the big picture window of Java Jane's Café where I worked, as well as any number from when I wasn't at work. Most of them were just image files on my computer, carefully named for what I remembered seeing when I took the shot. When I did take the time to reveal what I called a ghost image, I printed those files and kept them in a shoebox.

So far there weren't many photos in the box, but my apartment was filled with tons of reference books, print-outs from the Internet, and any other documentation I could track down on the weird and unexplained, including the odd tabloid newspaper. It made for a cluttered living space, but I knew where everything was.

"So do you do that a lot?"

I turned away from the window to see I had a customer waiting for me on the other side of the counter.

"I'm sorry," I said, stuffing my camera under the counter. "Can I take your order?"

"Sure," she said. "But you didn't answer my question."

"About...?"

"I was asking you if you did that a lot," she said. At my blank look, she added, "Take a picture like you just did, and then stare out the window as though there's something *really* interesting going by. Like a pig riding a unicycle, say. Or a parade of giant hamsters for Giant Hamster Pride Day."

I had to smile at the image that put in my head. Then I found myself wondering if maybe she saw the same strange things I did and I studied her for a moment.

I'd seen her come in earlier, but then I'd gotten distracted by the bear and its rider. She was wearing a sleeveless black T-shirt and camouflage cargos, and a pair of clunky platform shoes. Right now, the overhead lights in the café caught a hundred highlights in the mass of honey brown dreads she had piled up on her head like a Rasta beehive and her bright blue eyes contrasted sharply with her mocha skin, sparkling like a pair of sapphires. They were cheerful eyes, on the surface, but I could sense just a hint of some deep melancholy in them.

I knew about melancholy. It seemed my whole life carried an undercurrent of it, like the soundtrack to a slow-paced, serious foreign film. Seeing creatures that no one else could? That didn't help.

I wondered what my customer's excuse was. She didn't seem the sort of person to know the weight of too much sadness, but then you never knew, did you? I put her in her late twenties, maybe early thirties. Tall and slender, she'd navigated her way between the tables with a light grace that was a pleasure to watch, and she had a wonderful, open smile. But everyone has stories they keep hidden from the rest of the world. Everyone has secrets.

She was still waiting for my reply, so I shrugged.

"No," I said. "No hamsters or pigs. This was just a bear with a little man riding on its back. Though it might have been an otter. It was hard to tell."

Her eyebrows rose and she laughed. She had a good laugh—a kind of throaty chuckle.

"Oh-kay," she said, drawing the word out.

No, I realized then. She didn't see this sort of thing.

"So what can I get you?" I asked.

"Whatever you've been having."

I hadn't been sure before, but now it was obvious that she was flirting. I know a lot of places have rules against that sort of thing, but it's not like Java Jane's was some corporate coffee chain, with a head office handing down pronouncements from on high, and corporate managers making sure that said pronouncements were being followed. Duane McFarlane, who managed the café for the original Jane, was easygoing about…well, pretty much everything. He was good about making sure that the women who worked here didn't get hassled, and that they had rides home after a late shift, but how any of us interacted with the customers was our own business. Just so long as no one made a complaint.

But that wasn't about to happen right now, because there was no one here to complain. The flirting woman at my counter was my only customer, and Erin was out on the patio, bussing tables.

"What makes you think I've been having anything?" I asked. "Maybe I just have an innate ability to see things other people don't."

"I don't know," she said and then waited a beat. "Do you?"

Here's something I love: You can tell the truth, no matter how preposterous, and if it doesn't fit in with what the other person believes, they just think you're joking. But the nice thing about it—on the small karma scale—is that you don't have to lie when you're doing it.

"All the time," I told her.

"Like, what kinds of things?"

"You know that kid in *The Sixth Sense?*"

Her eyes widened theatrically. "You see *dead* people?"

"Not so much. More like weird people—or rather things that never were people. Fairies and goblins and things that go bump in the night. Though sometimes there are ghosts."

She took it all in stride, smiling as though we were sharing a joke.

"And how do you manage that?" she asked.

I smiled right back at her. "Do you have all day? Because I could bend your ear about it for hours."

She cocked her head for a moment—deciding something, I realized, when she reached out a hand to me.

"I'm Josie," she said.

Her hand was soft, but she had a firm shake.

"I'm Tom," I said. "Pleased to meet you, Josie."

"So what time do you get off work, Tom? You're allowed to date customers, right?"

I was enjoying this. It had been awhile since an attractive woman had actually paid any attention to me. It's not like I'm a total loser—though my friend Andrew might argue differently. I just hadn't had a date in awhile. Andrew says it's because I put out a "settled down" vibe, whatever that means.

"Are you asking me out?" I asked.

"What makes you think I would ask you out?"

"Because I'll be very disappointed if you aren't."

She gave me another one of those wonderful smiles of hers. "So, what time do you get off work?"

"See? You are asking me out."

"And you're avoiding my question again. Why is that? Are you married? Do you have a girlfriend?" She grinned. "Do you think I'm too pushy?"

"I'm single," I told her, "and we close at eleven, but I'm here until midnight or so. If you wanted to come by after eleven, we could talk while I'm cleaning up." I smiled and added, "And I don't think you're too pushy."

"I'll see you at eleven," she said.

"Don't you want your drink?" I asked as she started to turn away.

"Oh, right. I'll have a coffee and you'd better make it strong. I want to make sure I'm awake tonight."

A person could read all sorts of promise into a comment like that and be completely wrong.

I knew that. But as I watched her leave, weaving her way back through the tables with her coffee, I let the warm hope of promise fill me all the same. I didn't even try to take a picture of the little pack of spindly-limbed goblins I could see frolicking down the street when she opened the door.

And I didn't think again about that melancholy I'd seen so briefly in her eyes.

"So what do you do?" I asked Josie.

She'd come back, just a few minutes before eleven, still wearing her cargos and black T-shirt, but she'd added a jean jacket against the cooling evening air. I hadn't been sure she would actually return, but I was happy she had. When she'd stepped in through the front door, I'd called a cab for Erin, letting her go home so that Josie and I could have the place to ourselves. Erin had left with a teasing wink, but she was happy to be able to leave early.

Josie looked up now from where she was helping out, putting the chairs up on the tables while I cleaned the espresso machines.

"I'm in a band," she said.

"Really? What instrument do you play?"

"I don't. Well, I play a little guitar and I'm trying to learn the fiddle, but in the band I just dance."

She smiled at my confused look.

"It's step-dancing," she explained. "We're a Celtic band and I provide the percussion for the dance tunes."

"I don't know anything about Celtic music."

"Don't know, or don't care?"

"Well, more like I don't care for what I've heard. You know, in the pubs around town where everybody knows the words to these songs that sound really lame. Though what's that group that played for the Pope?"

"The Chieftains?"

I nodded. "I heard an album of theirs with a bunch of Nashville singers and I liked it."

"Well, we're not the Chieftains, but you should still come and see us sometime."

"I will. What's the name of your band?"

"Ballyogan—we got it from a reel our flute player loves. What about you? What do you do when you're not making a most excellent coffee or—" She paused for effect. "Taking pictures of things that nobody else can see?"

"When you put it like that..."

"You know what I mean."

I suppose I did. But it was a question I never knew how to answer. I was content enough with my life, but it wasn't exactly a stepping stone to greater things. It just was. I went to work. I read. I watched TV. Went to the movies. Hung out with friends. Spent probably way too much time researching weird fairy creatures or sitting at my computer, playing with images files in Photoshop.

"It wasn't supposed to be the kind of question that would stump you," she said.

"I know. It's just...I don't have a glamourous life. There's nothing special about me."

"Everybody's got something special about them," she said. "For instance, I can tap my head and rub my belly at the same time."

I smiled. "I don't have any such useful talent."

"Well, what about these things you can see that no one else can?" She pretended a sudden concern and looked around herself. "Are there any in here right now?"

Since I'd already told her about them, I decided to keep on being truthful—even if it just made her tease me more. Truth is, I didn't really mind her teasing. When she did it, she was laughing with me, not at me. At least she was so far.

"I don't usually see them indoors," I said. "Unless I'm in a museum or a library. Or down in the subway stations. They seem to like old public places. Oh, and malls. I'm always seeing them in shopping malls. I guess they like to shop."

We moved to one of the window tables now, taking a break, though the clean up was mostly done. She leaned across the table, her elbows on its surface as she cradled her chin in her hands. That bright blue gaze of hers settled on mine.

"So what exactly do you see?" she asked.

This was the moment, I realized. Up to now, it could all be put down to flirting and being silly. But this was the point where she would either think it was still charming, or decide I was a lunatic.

"Like I said before," I told her. "All sorts of things. Fairies and goblins. People that look like they're part animal and part human. Animals doing things that you wouldn't expect them to, like groundhogs riding skateboards, or a German shepherd on a bicycle. A giant once, but he was only fifteen or sixteen feet tall. I'd always thought they'd be bigger."

"Do you...see them all the time?" she asked.

"Only when they're around."

She sat back in her seat and nodded. "Of course."

This conversation wasn't going at all the way I'd expected it would. I'd rehearsed it a thousand times—not having it with Josie, just having it with someone, and it had never gone this far, or in this direction. Josie acted like we were talking about nothing more than the various customers who come into the café, or the people who live in my apartment building.

"So, have you always seen them?" she asked.

I shook my head. "No, only since I was around fifteen."

"And?" she said, making a "go on" motion with her hand.

"And what?"

"Did it just happen, or did something cause it to happen, or—well, what?"

I studied her for a long moment. "You really want to know?"

She nodded.

"I've never told this to anyone before."

"I'll tell you a secret, if you tell me yours," she said.

"I guess I can tell you."

Except then we just sat there for a few moments while I looked out the window and she looked at me. A skeleton in a white shirt and tie and a sharp black suit was walking by on the sidewalk. I'd seen him before and never could figure out how the bones all hung together.

"Are you just reluctant," she asked, "or can't you remember?"

"I can remember," I said, turning back to her. "It's not the kind of thing a person forgets."

I was fifteen when I came across a couple of dogs that had an old woman in a red hooded cloak backed up against the wall of an alleyway. I was taking a short cut on the way home from a video night at Andrew's house and stopped dead when I saw them.

Now, if you'd ever asked me what I'd do in a situation like this, I'd have told you that I would step right in and do the right thing. But in my heart, I knew I'd just run away. In my heart, I never lied to myself. I knew I was no hero. But I surprised myself that day. I picked up a garbage can and threw it at the dogs, yelling my head off. They scattered, one in either direction, but not before I'd clipped the biggest one with the edge of the can.

They stopped a half-dozen yards away and I grabbed another garbage can, though this time I didn't know which one I'd throw it at because they'd be coming at me from two directions.

You know how time does its weird thing in a situation like this? Everything slows down, but it's moving really fast at the same time. My pulse was drumming, thundering in my ears, but I still had time to note that the dogs were bigger and rougher looking than any I'd seen in the neighbourhood before. Almost wolfish. And they had a weird look in their eyes—a considering look that put the odd idea in my head that they were humans hidden in the skins of dogs.

One took a step forward—the big one, favouring a leg—and I stopped thinking stupid thoughts.

"Beat it!" I yelled, hoisting the can in its direction.

But I kept my eye on the other one.

I don't know how long we stood there like that—a few moments, a day—but suddenly, they just turned and trotted away, the big one limping. I lowered the garbage can, if not my guard.

"Are you okay?" I asked the old woman.

She was crouched on the ground, pressed up against the fence. I set the can down and went over to give her a hand up. I saw that the sleeve of her blouse was torn, but the skin didn't seem broken. Her hair was silver-grey, her face a roadmap of all the years she'd lived, but her eyes were bright and ageless.

"Did they hurt you?" I asked.

She shook her head.

"Where do you live?" I said. "You should let me walk you home."

"You're young to be so gallant," she said, "but I have no need of an escort now."

I remember thinking at the time that this was just an old person's way of talking.

"Um…right," I said. "But maybe you should still let me—"

"They never stop, you know," she said, interrupting me.

"Who doesn't?"

"The wolves."

I thought about the dogs that had attacked her and realized she'd confused them with wild animals. Sure, they'd looked wolfish, but we were in Upper Foxville, in the middle of the city, so what was the likelihood of running into a couple of actual wolves around here? Try zero.

"But they're not real wolves," she went on before I could say anything. "They're just cruel men, pretending to be wolves. That's all they've ever been. Real wolves don't toy with their prey. Real wolves offer a clean death to the weak and the old."

I was only fifteen, but I wasn't too young to know that she was probably off whatever meds she was supposed to be taking. Still, I remembered the strange human-like eyes of the dogs and, for a moment, I got this weird feeling as though I'd stepped into a dream. The air felt too thick, the ground spongy underfoot, and there was a sudden strong smell of cinnamon and cloves, here, then gone.

"I don't have much," the old woman said, "but I want to give you something for your aid."

"I don't need anything, ma'am. I was just happy to help."

She shook her head. "Kindnesses should never go unrewarded—especially when a reward is unlooked for. But I have so little now…"

"Please," I said. "It's reward enough to know that you're okay."

She smiled.

"Still the gallant," she said.

Then before I could move away, she reached out a hand, laying it on my brow. I closed my eyes when she drew it down my face. Her palm was soft as silk as it brushed against my eyelids.

"I have only this to give you," she said as she stroked my face. "The gift of Sight. I hope it will prove a boon to you, rather than a burden."

She said the word "sight" as though it had a capital letter at the beginning, as though it meant more than it would when you'd normally use the word.

And then…then I'm not sure what happened. One moment she was standing there in front of me, the next she took a step and disappeared as though she'd walked through an invisible door.

"Ma'am?" I called.

I moved to where she'd been standing, but no one was there. There was only the garbage can I'd thrown at the dogs, lying on its side, refuse pooling out of its mouth. No old woman. No dogs. No one.

Just me.

I don't know how long I stood there, but eventually I went on home. I didn't tell my parents about it, or anyone else. Partly because I didn't want to be seen like I was bragging—you know, with the rescuing bit. But it had also been so weird. If I told one part, I'd have to tell it all, and I knew how crazy it would sound, especially the way the old woman had simply upped and vanished.

But after that, I started seeing…*things*. And sometimes I felt as though maybe I was the one who was supposed to be on meds. But then I'd hear that old woman's voice in my head.

*I have only this to give you. The gift of Sight. I hope it will prove a boon to you, rather than a burden.*

And I came to realize that, impossible though it might seem, that was exactly what she'd done: given me an inside track into the unseen pieces of this world that most people don't get to witness.

The day I realized that I really wasn't going crazy was when I was walking by an art gallery on Waterhouse Street and I saw a painting in the window of this weird little elfish goblin man that I had actually seen out on the street just the week before. He'd been about two feet tall, dressed all in greens and browns, rooting through a garbage can for pop can tabs that he was making into a necklace. In the painting he was juggling two tin cans and a beer bottle.

I went inside the gallery and there were paintings of all sorts of the strange beings and creatures I'd been seeing—and many that I hadn't yet, though I did see some of them later.

I couldn't believe it, but here was the proof before me. Somebody else saw what I did.

I looked at Josie when I finished my story and was surprised at what I saw in her face.

"You half believe me," I said.

"Well, what do you expect? I'm Irish. We know about these things."

"You're Irish?"

"You never heard of the black Irish?"

I shook my head.

"How about Philip Lynott?"

I shook my head again.

"He was with Thin Lizzy."

"Oh, right."

"Black and Irish," she said.

"Does that mean you see this stuff, too?"

She shook her head. "But I've heard the stories growing up." She smiled. "It's a bit like a fairy tale, isn't it?"

"What do you mean?"

"Well, you help the old woman with the talking spoon and—"

"There was no talking spoon," I said. "At least not that time."

Her eyebrows went up. "You've *met* a talking spoon?"

"Not met, so much, as seen one. And heard it talking."

"To a fork."

"A saucer, actually."

A smile tugged at the corner of her mouth, but I could tell she still wasn't laughing at me, for all that it was pretty ridiculous, when you stopped to think about it. I mean, really. A spoon having a conversation with a saucer.

Except I'd heard that conversation. They'd been gossiping about someone that, naturally, I didn't know, but she sounded like a real firecracker, as my uncle used to say.

"So did you meet the artist whose work you saw in that gallery?" she asked.

I shook my head. "What was I going to do? Walk up to her and say, 'Hey, I've seen all those weird creatures, too'?"

"I guess not. Though maybe she could have helped you…I don't know, understand what you're seeing."

"I know what I'm seeing. That isn't the problem. The problem is that no one else can see them."

"And if they could?"

I shrugged, then sat back in my chair. "I don't know. I've been trying to take pictures of them. I see them fine through the viewfinder, but nothing ever shows up afterwards, except when I play around with the image in Photoshop, and even then it's hit and miss."

"You have pictures of them?"

"Not really," I said. "They're more like suggestions of what I saw. Ghost images."

She didn't say anything for a long moment. Her gaze went out the window to where two fat stubby figures with toad heads were walking by, arguing with each other, but I don't think she saw them.

"I'm just wondering," she said, turning back to me, "if maybe you aren't supposed to do something with this gift the old woman gave you."

I had no answer for that.

"I was wondering about something, too," I said instead. "Earlier today, why were you so…" I looked for a word and settled on, "forward with me?"

She laughed. "I don't think I've ever heard that expression used outside of a Romance novel."

"You know what I mean."

"I do." Her features went more serious. "It's because you seemed interesting and I've promised myself to always explore interesting things when they present themselves, otherwise they could go away and then I might find myself regretting the missed chance."

I would have preferred "handsome," or "sexy," but I could certainly live with "interesting." It was better than "dull."

I nodded my head to show I was listening. "Okay. So then…"

"My brother died of AIDs," she said.

"Oh, I'm really sorry."

"I am, too. I took care of him for the last year of his life. He said something to me, one day near the end, that I'll never forget. 'Don't live with regrets,' he told me. 'I have so many. So many things I wished I'd said, or done, or experienced, and now I never will. So when the opportunity arises, take hold of it and don't let it go.'"

Now I knew where that melancholy I'd seen earlier came from.

"He sounds like he was a brave guy," I said.

"He was scared out of his mind—right up until the last couple of months. After that, it was…strange. He got this amazing serene Buddha-like energy, like he knew what was coming and it was something good." She leaned forward again. "By the way, don't think I didn't notice how you avoided my question again. You'd make a terrible politician."

"What question?"

"This old woman gave you a gift," she said. "Don't you think you're supposed to use it?"

"To do what? I see weird things. That's the start and end of it. There doesn't seem to be anything I can do with what I see."

"But there must be some reason…"

"Maybe I'm just crazy."

"Maybe." She smiled. "But you're too cute to hide away someplace in a straitjacket."

That made me feel good. "Cute" was much better than "interesting."

"What I don't understand," she went on, "is how you don't even seem to like it."

"I didn't at first," I said. "Now…well, it's better than having a tooth pulled, but not so good as having a beautiful woman come into the café and flirt with me."

"Does that happen to you a lot?" she asked, eyebrows lifting.

"Hardly."

"Well, I'd love to be able to see into the otherworld. All the fairies and elves and ghosts and all."

"Maybe you can," I said. I'd thought about this before. "You know how sometimes a dog or a cat will become very interested in a section of wall, or a corner of a room, but there's nothing there that you can see?"

She nodded.

"Well, I read somewhere," I said, "that if you put your chin on their head when that happens, and look where they're looking, you can see it, too."

She studied me for a long moment.

"Have you tried this with anybody before?" she asked.

"Are you kidding? I haven't *told* anybody about it—not even Andrew, and we've been friends since grade school."

"But you've told me."

"It's more like you pulled it out of me. And as for Andrew, he'd rag me mercilessly for pretty much forever."

"Well, I'm game to try it," she said.

I looked out the window. A really creepy shambling cross between a great ape and sewer rat was going through the café's garbage bin at the corner of the patio. I waited until it was gone and there were only a few fairies fluttering like moths around the lamp of the streetlight outside before I turned back to Josie.

"Okay, stand behind me," I said, "and put your chin on my head."

She did as I said, her arms wrapped around me, her breasts pressed against my shoulders, the light scent of her perfume sweet in my nostrils.

"You're just trying to cop a feel," she joked as she got into position.

"Right. I've got hands on my back. Look up there, at the top of the streetlight. Do you see them?"

There was a moment's silence.

"I see moths," she said.

"That's all? You don't see little winged people as well?"

"No."

She moved her chin back and forth on the top of my head as she spoke.

I looked elsewhere, then spotted a man with a dog's head looking in the window of the used bookstore across the street.

"Let's try something else," I said. "Look across the street. Right there in front of Barrett's Books."

She shifted a little to fit her line of sight to mine.

"What am I supposed to be seeing?" she asked.

"A man with a dog's head."

"I don't even see the man."

"Try harder."

There was another moment of silence and I could feel her concentration like a physical thing, but then she pulled away and sighed.

"This isn't going to work," she said.

When she sat down, it was on my side of the table, pulling her chair closer so that she could lean her shoulder against mine.

"It's so frustrating," she said. "Growing up, my grandparents on both sides of the family had all these stories about the fairies and ghosts, and I always so wanted to be able to see them. I'd sit quietly at the bottom of the garden for hours, or creep around the woods in the ravine behind our house, searching and searching."

"But you never saw anything?"

She shook her head. "The closest I've come is when I heard the *bean sidhe*—the night my brother died. At least that's what Granny Burns said it was when I told her about it."

"The banshee?" I repeated.

She nodded, then spelled out the Gaelic for me. "It really means 'she-fairy,' but most people think of it as the evil spirit who heralds a death in the family. Granny Burns said she'd heard it twice in the old country—once each for when her parents died."

"That sounds spooky. What does she look like?"

"I have no idea. I didn't see her. I only heard her. In the stories, she's a hag, or a crow. Sometimes a crow woman. But what still troubles me about that night is that I don't know for sure if it was the *bean sidhe* I heard, or my brother Brandon."

"Why would you think it was your brother?'

She pulled away so that she was facing me and her gaze could meet mine.

"I don't know," she said. "But if it was, it would mean dying wasn't passing over to some beautiful otherworld, and I hate the idea of that. What if, when he died, he was looking into some kind of hell, or understood in that moment that we just go into nothingness, and what I heard was his cry of despair?" She shivered. "You can't imagine what a terrible sound it was. And how awful it feels thinking that after all that suffering he had to endure while he was dying, that maybe…maybe there was no better place for him to go on to."

Her eyes welled with tears, so I pulled her head gently to my shoulder and comforted her as best I could. There was nothing I could say, but I could at least hold her and offer her the anchor of another human being's sympathy.

"What do you think it was?" she said into my shoulder.

"I…I'm sorry, Josie. I have no way of knowing."

She sat up and wiped her eyes on the sleeve of her shirt. I reached over and grabbed a napkin from the holder on the table and offered it to her.

"Of course you couldn't," she said after she'd blown her nose. She gave me a smile that was a little forced, then added in a bright voice, "Well, it's a good thing this isn't a date, because it would be a lousy first date, wouldn't it? And I doubt I'd be seeing flowers tomorrow."

"If this was a date," I told her, "it would be a perfect one."

She shook her head. "Boy, you must be desperate."

"No, I just like you."

She'd let down the Rasta beehive of her hair earlier and her dreads now hung in a wild profusion down her shoulders and back. I reached out and touched one.

"And I'm really curious," I added, "as to how you get your hair to do this."

She rubbed my short hair with her hand.

"Grow yours long enough and I'll teach you."

I laughed. "I don't think so. I look like an idiot with long hair."

"So do you have any prints of the pictures you took?" she asked.

I nodded. "But not here. They're at my apartment."

"Can we go see them?"

I didn't answer immediately, because I was thinking about what a mess the place was, but she misread my silence as reluctance.

"I'm sorry," she said. "I'm being pushy again, aren't I?"

"It's not that. It's just that the place is pretty much a disaster area."

She smiled. "Big surprise. You're a single guy."

"Whoa—stereotyping."

She raised her eyebrows.

"Okay, maybe not so much," I said, "since I don't know one guy who has a tidy place, except Timothy, and he's gay."

"Now who's stereotyping?"

I smiled and got up from the table.

"Just let me finish cleaning the machines," I said.

Ten minutes later we were walking to my apartment, Josie's hand in the crook of my arm. My building was just around the corner, which made it convenient for work, but at that moment, I wished it was on the other side of town so that our walk could last longer. It was one of those great, late summer nights that feel full of promise, and I wasn't even worried about running into any of my visions.

When I'm out on my own, I've perfected a way of walking that lets me dodge whatever fairy beings might be out on the sidewalk with me without looking like I'm shooting for John Clease's job in the Ministry of Silly Walks.

I don't have to dodge them. Much of the time we seem to be on slightly different planes of existence so that we can pass through each other instead of colliding, but I still don't like the idea of it.

But tonight was quiet for a change. Or at least it was for this short walk we were taking. We only ran into one gang of carousing dwarves and they were easy to avoid because most of them were off the sidewalk, walking along the tops of the parked cars like short, drunken acrobats.

When we got to my apartment building, I led the way up to the third floor and unlocked the door. My black and white cat Chester met us on the threshold, protesting loudly as soon as I had the door open.

"C'mon, Chester," I said. "You know I always work late on Thursdays."

"Can you understand what he's saying?" Josie joked.

"Yeah. He's hungry and he wants to be fed."

"Maybe he just wants pats," she said.

She bend down on one knee and reached out her hand to Chester.

"Careful," I said. "He doesn't really..."

My voice trailed off before I could finish. Chester either avoided whomever came over to visit, or harassed them. He'd hiss and growl, sometimes taking swipes at their legs with his claws. And he didn't like to be picked up. Most of the time, he didn't even like me picking him up. But he let Josie reach under his shoulders and hoist him up into her arms.

"Doesn't really what?" she asked.

She held Chester as casually as though they'd known each other forever, scratching the top of his head with an easy familiarity as she looked around the living room.

"I was going to say he doesn't really like people," I said, "but obviously you're the exception."

"I just get along with animals," she said.

We fed Chester, then sat at the dining room table where I spread out the contents of my keeper photo box for her to look through. She seemed disappointed and I couldn't really blame her.

"You were expecting more, weren't you?" I said.

She nodded. "I can see the shapes of the beings you were talking about, but they really are only suggestions, aren't they?"

"And not very convincing ones. I warned you they weren't very good."

"I know," she said. "It's not that."

She pushed the prints into the middle of the table and sat back in her chair.

"I'd just like to be able to see them, too," she said. "That's all."

I gathered up the photos and stuck them back into their shoebox.

"I wish I could help," I said, "but you can see how well I've been able to share what I see so far."

"Did you ever try to find that woman you rescued?" Josie asked.

"Not really. I kept an eye out for her, but…" I shrugged. "I'm guessing it's a much bigger world out there than anyone ever thought it was. Maybe more than one world."

"What about the other beings you *can* see? Do you ever talk to them?"

"I did that once," I said. "It didn't go so well."

I was a couple of years older by that point and had accepted that I probably wasn't crazy. I was just seeing things that other people couldn't.

There are more things in heaven and earth, Horatio, than are dreamt of in your philosophy, and all that.

But while I didn't feel comfortable trying to talk about it to anyone in my life, I still needed to understand what was going on. *What* I was seeing, if not why. I already knew the why. The grey-haired Little Red Riding Hood I'd rescued had done this to me because I'd helped her.

So I decided that if I didn't feel comfortable talking about it with friends or family, maybe one of the beings I kept seeing would be able to put it all in perspective for me.

I was careful. I waited until I saw one of the more whimsical beings on his own—rather than trying to strike up a conversation with some creature that was all teeth and sharp claws.

I didn't expect any trouble. He was just this little guy, skinny, maybe three feet tall, and all arms and legs. His face was round, with a wide infectious smile and round saucer eyes that gave him a look of constant startlement. I spied him sitting between the paws of one of the lions in front of the Newford Public Library, though I hadn't noticed him right away. He was wearing clothes that appeared to be made of leaves and vines and his hair was like a bird's nest. At first glance, I thought it was just a clump of seasonal debris, caught up between the paws. Then the clump moved and I saw the little man for what he was.

I looked around myself. The closest people were a bunch of high school kids at the bottom of the steps and they appeared to be too busy amusing each other to notice me talking to myself. Or at least what would appear to be me talking to myself.

I sat on my heels so that I wasn't towering over him.

"Um…hello?" I tried.

I thought at first that he was going to ignore me, but then those big saucer eyes focused their gaze on my own.

"Don't think for a minute," he said, "that being able to see me gives you any kind of power over me. I don't have three wishes, or a pot of gold, and even if I did, I wouldn't give them to a little pissant shite like you."

Then he grinned and I saw a mouthful of sharp barracuda teeth. I felt like I'd stuck my hand in a tank full of carp, only to discover that they were really piranha, and was too startled to even back away.

"I…I…" was the most I managed to get out.

"Practicing to be a pirate are we?" he said. "Well, piss off and do it somewhere else."

"No, I just…I didn't mean to bother you."

"And yet you won't stop."

This was so not going the way I'd hoped it would.

"I just wanted to know why I can see you," I said.

He put his hand on his chin pretending to think.

"Let's see," he said. "You've got yourself a pair of pluiking eyes. Could that be the reason why?"

"I mean, when nobody else can."

"Who gives a shite? Just piss off before I show you what these teeth do best."

He grinned again and this time I was able to scramble to my feet and make my retreat.

"Needless to say," I told Josie, "I've not been in any hurry to try that again."

"I don't blame you."

I looked around at the familiar confines of my living room. The overflowing bookcases, the papers stacked in unsteady piles, Chester asleep on the back of the sofa. Then my gaze went to Josie, sitting across the table from me.

"I can't believe you're here," I said. "I mean, that you're here and we're having this conversation."

She smiled. "It is an unusual conversation."

Her attractiveness was distracting, but not so much that I didn't find myself going back to puzzling over her easy acceptance of what I'd been telling her.

"Who are you really?" I asked.

Her brows went up in exaggerated surprise and she smiled that winning smile of hers.

"Josephine Ryan," she said. "A dancer in a Celtic group called Ballyogan. Who are you really?"

"You know what I mean. You just came into the café out of nowhere, taking every weirdness I've handed you in stride, without blinking an eye. I don't get it."

But then I had a thought.

"You're not that old woman, are you?" I asked. "Come back in disguise to make sure I was using my gift properly."

"Why would you think that?"

"Because that's how it happens in stories, and you're so damn calm about all of this, and you were asking me about why I wasn't using my Sight."

"Maybe I'm just a girl who got curious and now finds herself liking you way too much for the short time we've known each other."

"Do you?"

She nodded, her gaze steady as it held mine. "Weird as you are, I find there's this immediate connection and level of comfort with you."

I felt the same way. The connection part was easy to understand. Any guy is going to feel that way with the attentions of a good-looking woman upon him. But being so comfortable in her company was an entirely different and new thing. Never mind that this was a conversation that I'd never had before. What was strange was how normally I'd be feeling awkward and decidedly uncool in such intimate proximity to a woman such as her. But I didn't.

It was different in the café. There I found it easy to talk and flirt with the female customers. It was just for fun and it wasn't going to go anywhere. This wasn't the same at all. This—for all we'd only known each other for a few hours—had promise. And because of that, I wanted to do something for her.

"You're so quiet," she said.

"I was just thinking. About your brother."

"My brother...?"

I nodded. "Was he buried in the city?"

"Why would you want—" she began, but then she got it. "Do you really think you could talk to him?"

"I have no idea," I said. "But I could try."

The Oak Grove Cemetery wasn't far from my apartment. Far enough that we had to take a bus to the east end of Stanton Street, and then walk the last couple of blocks north, but it wasn't as though it was on the other side of town. Of course it was the last bus of the night, so we did have a long walk ahead of us to get back.

The cast-iron gates were locked. A pair of lion statues, one on each of the gate's pillars, ignored us as I boosted Josie up so that she could grab the upper railings and climb over them. I followed after her, jumping down the last few feet with my knees bent to absorb the shock.

"Which way?" I asked her.

She pointed down the central path.

"I've never been here at night," she said as we walked hand in hand along the path. "It's not spooky like I thought it would be. It's so peaceful."

It was. As we'd made our way here, I'd seen a fair amount of otherworldly creatures cavorting about on the streets—there always seemed to be more, later at night like this—but the graveyard itself was quiet. No fairies, no goblins. Not even any ghosts—or at least none that were obvious.

I had no idea if this was going to work. So far as I could tell, most spirits didn't stick around as ghosts. Those that did stay on to haunt the living world had never appeared very communicative to me. Whenever I saw them, they were usually insubstantial and disengaged from the world, drifting aimlessly around. But I wanted to try this for Josie's sake. It would be nice to have this ability of mine actually be useful for a change.

"I can't promise anything will happen," I said, voicing my worry for about the tenth time since we'd left my apartment.

"I know," Josie said. "But in some ways, it already has."

"How so?"

"Just knowing that ghosts exist means that *something* goes on after we die. That's already a comfort."

Maybe so, but I wanted to do more. I wanted this weird gift of mine to actually prove to be worthwhile, instead of just endlessly distracting.

We had to leave the main path to reach her brother's gravesite. He had a modest stone, shaded from the direct moonlight by one of the enormous oaks that had given the cemetery its name. It bore his name and the dates of his birth and death. I did a rapid calculation and realized that he'd been younger than me when he'd died. That so sucked. I didn't come close to having my life in any sort of order, and here he'd already died.

Josie bent down and straightened the flowers that were in a small stone vase in front of the stone. She ran her fingers across his name, then looked up at me.

"Is he here?" she asked.

"I don't see him," I said. "I haven't seen anyone since we climbed over the gates."

Except then I did. He was sitting on a moonlit stone a few graves over, a small figure in old-fashioned clothing and a leather flight jacket. I thought he was bald until I realized he was wearing a close-fitting aviator's leather cap, the straps dangling on either side of his face. I didn't think he was a ghost because he was so present, but I wasn't sure if he was a magical being either, because he looked so human. So normal. Except for that cap and flight jacket, which seemed out of place, and out of time.

He tapped a finger against his forehead by way of greeting when he saw me looking his way.

"What is it?" Josie asked, her gaze following mine, but there was nothing there for her to see. "Is it Brandon?"

I shook my head.

"I don't know who or what it is," I said.

"But you see something."

I nodded. "Wait here a moment."

I left her by her brother's grave and walked over into the moonlight to where the man sat, his heels tapping against the gravestone under him. As

I got closer to him, I realized that he was actually a she. I thought she looked familiar, then realized it was because she reminded me of the singer Ani DiFranco—if DiFranco was channeling Amelia Earheart, that is.

"Don't think I've ever heard someone refer to me as an 'it' before," the woman said as I approached.

"I'm sorry. I didn't mean it like that. It's just…are you a ghost, or something else?"

"Probably something else," she said, but she didn't elaborate any further. "There was a time I answered to Emaline."

It was a funny way to put it, but I'd come across a lot of references in my research about how beings from the otherworld were cagey with their real names.

"I'm Tom," I said and offered her my hand.

She seemed surprised by the gesture but she shook, her palm dry and raspy against mine. For my part, this was so different from the encounter I'd had with the little man and his mouthful of sharp teeth, that I was determined to be polite and show that I was appreciative of the fact that Emaline was actually talking to me.

"This is interesting," she said as she let go of my hand. "People don't usually see me unless I want them to."

"I have this thing."

"The Sight."

I nodded.

"And how's that working out for you?" she asked.

"It complicates my life a little, but otherwise it's fine."

"Yeah, it'll do that," she said. Her gaze went past me to Josie. "Your girlfriend's a real keeper. I've seen her come to that grave before."

"It's a little early to call her a girlfriend, but she's sure something else."

"And the grave?"

"It's her brother's."

Emaline nodded thoughtfully, as though I'd just said something profound.

"So what are the two of you doing here?" she asked. "Seems kind of late at night to be paying your respects."

"I was hoping to help her," I said and started to explain.

Josie came up as I was finishing and my heart sank a little when I saw the worried way she was looking at me. She'd been willing to go this far, but standing by while I conducted a conversation with what seemed like no more than the night air, had to really be stretching her credulity.

"I wish she could see you," I told Emaline. "I wish she could see all of you. The fairies and goblins and skeleton men and all."

"What's stopping her?"

"I don't understand."

"Why do you See?"

"I helped an old lady—an old fairy lady, I guess—and she gave me the gift."

"So why don't you do the same?"

I just looked at her for a long moment.

"It's that easy?" I asked, remembering how the old woman had simply stroked my face, soft fingers butterfly light on my eyelids.

"It helps if it's something she really wants," Emaline said. "And it's always easier with someone who already has a yearning for the otherworld."

"Except I didn't have either."

"Oh no?" she asked with arched eyebrows. "Then how did you see an old fairy woman?"

"I…"

I'd never thought about that before.

"Who are you talking to?" Josie asked.

I turned to her. "This woman…"

"What's she saying?"

"That I can make you see her—all of them—if you really want to."

"I do." Before I could ask her if she was sure, she added, "Has she…seen my brother?"

"Stand still for a moment," I said instead of answering her. "And close your eyes."

I tried to remember the exact words the old woman had used, then decided it didn't really matter. They were too simple to have been a spell. It had more to do with intent and, in Josie's case, her desire.

"Think of having the Sight," I told her.

"I don't—"

"Just try to concentrate on that one thing," I said.

Then I laid my hand on her brow and drew my hands lightly down over her eyes, the way the old woman had.

"I give you the gift of the Sight," I said.

I felt a little stupid, saying it out loud like that, but I did it anyway, focusing on her being able to See the way that I could.

It seemed such a little thing to do. Surely there had to be more. Incantations and power and complicated magical gestures. But it was all I had.

"Okay," I said. "You can look now."

Her eyes opened and went wide when she saw Emaline sitting on the gravestone in the moonlight.

"Oh my god," she said in a very small voice. Then her hand went up to her mouth and she added, speaking to Emaline, "I'm sorry. I know we're not supposed to say that to one of your kind."

Emaline laughed. "Where do you people get these ideas? Jesus Christ. Mother Mary. The Pope and all his cardinals. There. You see? Doesn't affect me at all."

"You—you're not a fairy?" she said.

Emaline avoided her question as deftly as she had mine.

"Most of you don't believe what you read in the tabloids," she said, "so why do you believe what you read in a fairy tale?"

Josie nodded, immediately getting it. For my part, I just felt a little dumb for all the time I'd been "researching" those very sources.

"And besides," Josie said. "A lot of those stories were written by the devout, and you're much older than that, aren't you? The otherworld's been close at hand since before Jesus was even born, so why should the mention of his name cause you any discomfort?"

I regarded her with admiration. Unlike me, at least she was smart. And she'd adjusted to being able to see a formerly invisible woman as readily as she'd listened to me. She really was something.

"Now we can ask her about your brother," I said, "and I don't have to pass the answer on to you secondhand."

"You've seen my brother?" Joise asked, her voice eager.

"No," Emaline said. "But it's not like I'm here twenty-four-seven or anything."

I could feel Josie deflate beside me and took her hand. She squeezed my fingers, but didn't take her gaze from Emaline.

"You have to understand," Emaline added, "that most spirits just go on. A new journey lies ahead of them and they're eager to take the road that we can't follow until we die."

"Is it to a better place?"

"I don't know," Emaline said. "It's to another place. That's all anyone knows, really. There are places where spirits tarry—here and in the other-worlds—but sooner or later, everyone goes on. You shouldn't be in such a hurry to find out. You still have your life ahead of you."

"I know. It's just…I was with him when he died and I heard this terrible wailing sound. My grandmother said I'd heard the *bean-sidhe,* but…what if I didn't? What if he's suffering? What if there's nothing after us when we die—just some great horrible void?"

Emaline regarded her for a long moment.

"I think that's why you people have religions," she finally said. "It allows you the comfort of believing that there's a point to everything, when really, the world just is, and we live in it until we don't."

"That's kind of harsh," I said.

"I suppose it could be taken that way," she said, "but I don't mean that there's no point to living. It's just that, where we came from, where we go—maybe these are the mysteries we're not supposed to know. Maybe we're supposed to be paying attention to the lives we have and the world we are in."

"But—"

"And that, I think," she said before Josie could even start her next question, "is maybe why we have each other. Because in the here and now, we only have each other. That's all we really have that we can count on."

"So…it's not something we can ever really know," Josie said.

Emaline shook her head. "It's not something we even need to know—not until it's time for us to go on ourselves. I know you miss your brother. We all miss the ones who go on and leave us behind. I don't think that ever stops. But our concern is the business of living."

Josie sighed. "I guess. But just carrying on—it's an easier thing to say than it is to do."

"Not if we're doing it right," she told her. "Leave the dead to their journeys, and put your attention on the ones that you take."

She gave us a toothy smile and tipped her finger against her brow the way she had when I'd first noticed her.

"Just think of all you'll miss if you don't," she said.

And then she was gone, just like the old lady had disappeared on me all those years ago, except she didn't even step away. She simply did a Cheshire Cat fade, leaving nothing of herself behind. Not even a grin.

Still holding my hand, Josie turned to me.

"Did I really see that?" she asked.

I nodded. "And since you saw that, there's a whole world of things you're going to see from here on out."

"It's a little scary, isn't it? I mean, I've wanted this forever, but now…now it feels a little scary."

"It doesn't have to be. I'll be here for you. Like Emaline said—we have each other."

She cocked her head. "But you haven't even kissed me yet."

So I did.

When we reached the entrance to the cemetery, Josie turned around before we could climb back over the gates. She stood there for a long time, looking out across the field of gravestones and the tall oak trees that loomed over them.

"Thinking of your brother?" I said.

She nodded. "I know Emaline said we shouldn't focus on that kind of thing, but it's hard not to. Does my believing he's okay make it happen? Is it enough?"

It'll have to be, I thought, but I didn't say it aloud. I didn't need to. I could see in her eyes that she knew it was all she had. That, and her memories.

I gave her a leg up and we climbed over the ironwork until we were on the other side of the gates. Josie did a double-take as a riderless bicycle went wheeling by, its fat rubber tires whirring on the pavement.

"Did you see that?" she asked.

I smiled and nodded. "And what about that?"

I pointed across the street to where a gang of small fairies that looked like they were made of twigs and leaves were playing some sort of a game with an empty plastic jug. They would kick it like a soccer ball, swarming each other as they tried to—well, I'm not sure what the point of the game was. But they were certainly having fun with it. Watching the game from their side of the street was a figure with a beehive for a head.

"This has been an amazing night," Josie said when she finally turned back to me. "Though it's funny, our meeting that strange fairy woman in the graveyard, just when we did."

"Not really," I said. "That's something that comes up again and again in my research into all of this. The idea of synchronicity. How things just seem to connect, once you put your foot on a certain path."

"Like our meeting in the café."

I nodded. "That would be the start of it."

"I'm glad we met," she said.

"Because now you can See?"

She took my hand and gave me a tug.

"No," she said as we walked down the street, the echoing laughter of the little twig people fading behind us. "It's because for the first time since Brandon died, I don't feel so alone anymore."

Then before I could wonder if she only saw me as a brother, she twirled around until she was facing me. Putting her arms around my neck, she gave me a long kiss and all my worries went spinning away.

I thought I heard something then—but I couldn't quite place it. Maybe the distant sound of an old prop plane, or an acoustic guitar played with a very percussive attack. Or it could have been the sound of my own pulse, drumming in my ears. I felt an empty place inside me fill up with possibilities and I realized I didn't feel alone anymore either except, unlike Josie, I hadn't realized just how much I'd been feeling that way.

Then I stopped trying to analyze everything the way I always do and took Emaline's advice. I let myself expand into the moment until it was the only thing I was experiencing.

With Josie's lips on mine, her arms around me and her body pressed close, it was a perfect moment.